The four girls whirled around the room, pushing their trays under the guests' noses and looking so pleading that nearly every guest found themselves taking a canapé whether they wanted one or not. Jas was getting more and more agitated, and when she saw that the other three had all emptied their platters, she hurriedly shoved her last three blinis in her mouth and hurried over to join them.

But as they turned to leave, a terrible scream rang out.

The girls spun round. It was Olivia Fortune who had screamed. People were rushing towards her, but it wasn't Olivia they were looking at.

'It's Mr Fortune!' cried Becky. 'He's collapsed!'

www.kidsatrandomhouse.co.uk

Also available in

The Mayfair Mysteries

series:

# The Mayfair Mysteries

Alex Carter



RED FOX

THE MAYFAIR MYSTERIES: THE CASE OF THE POISONED PIE
A RED FOX BOOK 978 1 849 41172 1

Published in Great Britain by Red Fox Books,
an imprint of Random House Children's Books
A Random House Company

This edition published 2011

3 5 7 9 10 8 6 4

Series created and developed by Amber Caravéo

Cover illustration by Katie Woods



The Random House Group Limited supports The Forest Stewardship Council (FSC®), the leading international forest certification organisation. Our books carrying the FSC label are printed on FSC® certified paper. FSC is the only forest certification scheme endorsed by the leading environmental organisations, including Greenpeace. Our paper procurement policy can be found at www.randomhouse.co.uk/environment

Set in Stempelschriedler

Red Fox Books are published by Random House Children's Books,
61–63 Uxbridge Road, London W5 5SA

www.**kids**at**randomhouse**.co.uk

Addresses for companies within The Random House Group Limited can be found at:
www.randomhouse.co.uk/offices.htm

THE RANDOM HOUSE GROUP Limited Reg. No. 954009

A CIP catalogue record for this book is available from the British Library.

Printed and bound by CPI Group (UK) Ltd, Croydon, CR0 4YY

With special thanks
to Jacqueline Rayner

# Lauren

**Eye colour:** blue

**Hair:** auburn – like the rest of the family – cut into a bob

**Style:** jeans, T-shirts and Converse

**Siblings:** Charlie, an annoying little brother

**Likes:** anything sporty, especially swimming in the lush hotel pool

**Dislikes:** tidying her room

**Prize possession:** mobile phone, for keeping the other girls up to date with all the action at the Mayfair Park

**Dreams of:** running her own chain of luxury hotels, one in LA, New York, Paris, Dubai . . . a home on every continent!

# Jas

**Eye colour:** brown

**Hair:** shoulder length, Afro-Caribbean curls

**Style:** glam and wild! Favourite items include super-sparkly shoes and anything with animal print

**Likes:** spending time with her BFFs

**Dislikes:** sitting still, Maths lessons, sitting still in Maths lessons . . .

**Secret talent:** impressive acting skills – useful in getting the girls out of several sticky situations with The Snoop

**Dreams of:** becoming the next Beyoncé or Tyra Banks – Jas is definitely the diva of the group!

# Mia

**Eye colour**: brown

**Hair**: very long, very dark, shiny and straight

**Style**: eclectic – Mia mostly wears bright colours, layered with one of her mum's vintage Spanish scarves

**Siblings**: two geeky older brothers

**Likes**: all animals, especially those in need of some TLC

**Prize possession**: a top-of-the-range laptop – Google can help solve almost any mystery!

**Dreams of**: working for the United Nations, or becoming a vet

# Becky

**Eye colour**: grey
**Hair**: blonde, shoulder-length curls
**Style**: pretty and girly . . . floaty skirts, floral tops and high heels
**Likes**: organising things for everyone, especially her forgetful dad . . . and chocolate!
**Dislikes**: untidiness – the total opposite of super-messy Lauren!
**Prize possession**: her collection of celeb memorabilia. The Mayfair Park is the perfect place for celeb-spying . . .
**Dreams of**: being a high-flying celebrity agent – Becky was born super-glam and super-organized!

# CHAPTER ONE

'Time to get up, Lauren!' called Mum.

Lauren Bond groaned and stumbled out of bed. She picked up her school skirt from where it was lying crumpled on the floor, and looked around for a shirt. She was just about to yell to her mum to ask for a clean one, when she remembered. It was the first day of the summer holidays! She could sleep all day!

With a yawn, Lauren went back to her comfy bed. Her head hit the pillow and her eyes closed.

'Lauren! Rise and shine! There's a surprise waiting in the kitchen!' That was Mum again.

There was really nothing for it but to get up. Lauren pulled a dressing gown on over her night-shirt and opened the bedroom door. A blur in bright red robot pyjamas sped past, its nose in the air. This was Charlie, Lauren's younger brother, acting like a dog following a scent. A few seconds later, the scent hit Lauren's nose too – pancakes! Mum's pancakes were famous in the Bond household – they were the American sort that came in huge piles with maple syrup and blueberries and cinnamon. If that was the surprise, it was worth giving up a lie-in for. Breakfast most days was toast and cereal as neither of Lauren's parents had much time to spend on cooking. Her dad was manager of the Mayfair Park, a luxury London hotel, and her mum was the head of hospitality. Their jobs could go on from early in the morning to late at night, and on every day of the week too.

At least they didn't have a long journey to work, though – the Bond family lived in their own flat in a wing of the hotel, complete with bedrooms, lounge, bathroom, and of course the kitchen that Lauren was now running towards, her sleepiness forgotten at the thought of food.

She stopped dead in the doorway.

There on the table were five enormous piles of pancakes. Charlie had already claimed one of them, and happily tucking into three of the others were Lauren's best friends, Jas, Mia and Becky.

'Surprise!' said Mrs Bond, who was washing up an enormous frying pan.

'Wow, did you lot forget it was the holidays

too?' Lauren asked, taking a seat behind the final pancake stack. 'I mean, how early is this?'

Jas's eyebrows shot up. 'Wake up, Lols! Today's the day!'

'Yeah, first day of the holidays, I know—'

'Lauren,' said Becky pityingly, 'it's 4ever day!'

'Oh!' Lauren's mouth dropped open as the others burst out laughing. Of course! The new boyband 4ever were filming their first video in the hotel!

'Becky texted us all to wake us up, then her dad drove us here,' Mia explained. 'We didn't want to miss any of it.'

'I texted you too,' Becky told Lauren.

Lauren wrinkled her nose. 'Well, I expect my phone's *somewhere* in my room . . .'

Becky groaned, as Lauren knew she would. 'If only you'd let me tidy up a bit . . .'

'Oh, Rebecca, I wish you could!' Mrs Bond called over from the sink. 'But Lauren'd mess it up again within minutes.'

'Mum!' Lauren cried, embarrassed. It was true, though. Somehow she just couldn't keep things neat – and somehow she just couldn't see that it mattered, really. Becky was a bit of a neat freak, but then she was used to tidying up after her absent-minded-professor father since her mother had died a few years ago.

The piles of pancakes in front of the four girls rapidly disappeared. 'The video's being shot in the spa,' Jas told Lauren. 'Your mum's spoken to the director and she says we can watch, as long as we stay well out of the way and don't bother anyone.'

'And you must leave if they ask you to,' Mrs Bond put in. 'It's my day off and I don't want to be called down to deal with any problems.'

'Yes, Mum,' said Lauren, and 'Yes, Mrs Bond,' chorused the others. They knew they were lucky that Lauren's mum and dad let them hang around the hotel so much – to the dismay of Mrs Stoop the housekeeper – and were careful not to make a nuisance of themselves.

Lauren checked she'd managed to scrape every last drop of maple syrup from her plate, then jumped up. 'Come on, then,' she said. 'To the spa! What are we waiting for?'

The others didn't move. 'Er, I think we're waiting for you to change out of your nightshirt?' suggested Mia, grinning.

Ten minutes later, the four girls were heading down in the staff lift, Lauren now dressed in shorts and T-shirt. 'Lauren, we're going to meet *a band*!' said Jas. 'What'd it take for you to put on something a bit *girlie*?!'

'I dunno – a blue moon or something?' suggested Lauren.

Jas shook her head in disbelief. She loved getting dressed up and couldn't understand why it didn't interest Lauren at all. She and Becky had spent ages choosing their band-meeting wardrobes – a pink strappy top and a short layered skirt made out of cream lace with strappy pink sandals for Jas, and a blue and white stripy dress with a belt and embroidered pumps for Becky. Jas thought that if *she* lived somewhere as elegant as the Mayfair Park Hotel, she'd have to wear her best clothes every day!

On the ground floor of the hotel was a large heated swimming pool, a curved swirly shape that looked a bit like a chubby question mark with a round Jacuzzi pool making the dot at the bottom. The blue tiles on the floor of the pool and the potted palms around the sides – as well as the always balmy atmosphere – gave the place a Mediterranean feel. Normally there would be at least two or three guests either in the water or relaxing on the blue-and-white-striped loungers that surrounded the pools, but today a RESERVED notice at the entrance meant that it was empty.

The far wall of the pool room was all glass, with glass doors leading into the reception area of the spa. This was a large, wooden-floored space, normally full of comfortable armchairs and low tables where guests would sip at healthy mineral waters while waiting to be ushered into one of the individual treatment rooms for a massage, a manicure or a mud-pack.

Today, however, the chairs and tables had all been cleared. The marble-topped desk, normally manned by either Marie or Judith, the spa receptionists, stood empty. The leafy palms in their terracotta pots, however, were still in their places – and had been joined by about a hundred more. There were vines hanging from the domed roof, and the floor was carpeted with flower petals of red, pink and yellow. Tall lamps threw out a bright golden light.

From the pool room, the girls gazed through the glass wall into the spa.

'Wow,' gasped Jas. 'Is that London or Hawaii?'

'It's beautiful,' said Mia.

'Stunning,' added Becky.

Lauren just stared, open-mouthed.

Even though the girls were used to the luxurious surroundings of the Mayfair Park, this was something else. It was just like a tropical rainforest. Jas wouldn't have been surprised to see parrots flying from tree to tree, or a monkey swinging through the vines.

They pulled four of the pool-room loungers closer to the glass wall so they could see what was going on in the spa next door. They didn't have a brilliant view because of all the plants dotted around, but at least they wouldn't be in anyone's way.

'It's like being a spy,' said Mia, peering round a potted palm at the cameramen setting up their equipment.

'You sound like Charlie!' said Lauren.

'Is he still introducing himself to people as *Bond – Charles Bond*?' asked Becky, putting on a deep voice that made the others laugh.

Lauren nodded. 'Yes. It's *sooo* embarrassing.'

'Anyway,' put in Jas, 'we're not spies – we're detectives.'

Mia looked surprised. 'Is there something to detect, then?'

'Well, no – but we did solve a huge mystery last term, didn't we? That officially makes us detectives.'

'"Schoolgirl detectives", they said in the papers,' Becky pointed out.

'And they called it "The Case of the Ruby Necklace",' Lauren said. 'That sounds so cool. I've been reading loads of detective stories, and you always have to give each case a cool name.'

'Well, how about "The Case of the Gorgeous Guys" for this one?' Jas said, nudging Lauren hard. 'Look! Is that them?'

Four young men had just arrived. Sadly for the girls, they hadn't entered the spa through the pool room, but had come through a separate door on the far side of the reception area. They wore swimming trunks and brightly patterned Hawaiian shirts.

Mia followed Jas's gaze and nodded. 'That's 4ever!' she said. 'I looked them up on the Internet. The one on the left with blond hair is Pete – he likes travelling and chocolate. Then that one's Jason and he likes scary films. Niall is the one with red hair, and he likes football, tennis and swimming, and the one on the end is Robin, who has three horses and goes riding whenever he can.'

'That is so spooky!' said Jas.

The others frowned. 'What is?'

'Well, they're just like us! Becky is blonde and likes chocolate—'

'We all like chocolate!' put in Mia.

Jas wasn't put off. 'Lauren is sporty, and she has red hair—'

'Auburn!' said Lauren.

'Well, reddish, then.' Jas continued, 'Mia loves animals, and Jason and I have really similar names, Jason and Jasmine.'

'And you like scary films – all that ghost rubbish!' added Becky.

'Uh-huh,' agreed Jas – she was too excited to argue with Becky about her lack of taste. 'Well – what d'you think? I reckon we should form a rival girl band!'

The others laughed. 'I think you have to be able to sing as well,' Lauren said, 'and my singing sounds like one of Mia's cats caught in the rain.'

'Talking of cats,' Becky said, turning to Mia, 'how are the kitten twins?'

Mia beamed happily. 'They've both got new homes!' she said.

The others smiled too. Animal-loving Mia had rescued two orphaned kittens whose mother had been run over. Not only had she taken them to a shelter, she'd kept visiting and helped to feed them with bottles of milk until they were ready to be re-homed.

'You'll miss going to the shelter now the kittens have gone, won't you?' Lauren asked.

Mia looked a bit sheepish. 'Well . . .' she said, 'there's this little dog at the shelter, he's called Tumble . . .'

Becky, Jas and Lauren almost forgot about 4ever in their eagerness to find out more about Tumble. They always loved hearing about Mia's latest rescue project, even though none of them were quite as animal-mad as their friend.

Mia explained that Tumble had hurt his leg, but now it was healed he needed to get lots of exercise, so she was taking him for walks. 'The worst thing is,' said Mia, 'that even when he's better, he'll probably never get a proper home, because he might always have a limp and he's quite old, and people only want to adopt cute puppies. But he's the most loveable dog in the world – apart from Benjie, of course.' Benjie was Mia's own dog.

'Can't he live with you?' asked Jas.

Mia shook her head. 'Mum says one dog is enough. And anyway, Tumble doesn't really get on with cats – he barks his head off whenever he sees one.' As well as Benjie the Labradoodle, Mia had two tabby cats, Arthur and Guinevere. She also had several rabbits!

There was a shout from the spa: 'Quiet please, everyone!' Although the girls were pretty sure they couldn't be heard from where they were sitting in the pool room, they all stopped talking. Anyway, they were too excited to speak. Filming was about to begin!

Hours went by. The girls were hot and thirsty, but none of them dreamed of leaving. It was still so exciting – they were only a few metres away from 4ever, even if there was a glass wall between them! Luckily the music was loud enough for them to hear everything clearly. They were enjoying themselves so much that hearing the band sing the same tiny bit of the song again and again and again while the director shot it in different ways and from different angles didn't bother them in the slightest.

In fact, Becky suddenly noticed that even Lauren was humming along with the chorus. 'I thought you didn't sing!' she said.

'I don't,' Lauren answered. 'I didn't realize what I was doing! It's just so catchy!'

Just then Tom, one of the hotel's waiters, walked past them. He was carrying a tray with four tall glasses of fresh lemonade, each one full of ice cubes and with a slice of lemon floating on top. 'Oh, please let those be for us . . .' Jas said, sticking out her tongue and pretending to be dying of thirst. Becky agreed – she felt like she really was in a tropical rainforest!

''Fraid not,' said Lauren, laughing, as Tom went through the glass doors into the spa and handed out the drinks to the 4ever boys. As he came back into the pool room, Lauren beckoned to him from round a potted palm. He spotted her and changed course, coming over to them.

'Tom! Tom! Did you speak to them?' demanded Jas.

Tom grinned. 'I certainly did,' he said. 'Ooh, we had quite a chat. I asked if they would like a nice cool drink . . . and they said they would.'

'Wow,' said Jas. Becky smiled to herself. If Jas thought that was exciting, she'd probably explode if she ever got to speak to the band! Not that it was likely. The girls had promised to keep their distance.

'You should have given them your CD,' she said to Tom.

The young man blushed. 'They wouldn't be interested in that,' he said.

Jas jumped up. 'Oh, Tom, you've got to! You're so good! Everyone at school's watched your YouTube video – it's got thousands of hits.'

'Two thousand, three hundred and eight, last week, anyway,' put in Mia. 'And that's loads if you've not been on telly or anything. It means you've got lots of fans.'

'So you've just got to let the music people hear you sing,' Lauren completed.

But Tom was looking really shy. 'They'd laugh at me,' he said. 'It's different, just playing to friends or putting something on the Internet, but I couldn't talk to important record people.' The four girls hastened to reassure him, but Tom was adamant.

'Hold on a minute!' Jas suddenly cried. 'I've got a plan!' The others turned to her expectantly. Jas could always be relied on to come up with ideas. 'We put Tom's CD on the hotel's public address system!' she said. 'Then all the record people will hear it. They'll ask who that brilliant singer is, we'll say "Oh, don't you know? That's Tom McQueen," and they'll say "Wow, really?" and then they'll sign him up! Sorted.'

'Or they'll say "Turn that racket off!" and we'll all get into trouble with Lauren's mum and dad!' said Tom. He smiled at the girls. 'It's really good of you, all of you. But I'm happy with my job, and you know what? I think I'll stay being a waiter – well, for today anyway. Talking of which, can I fetch any of you young ladies a cool drink?'

'Oh, Tom, that would be brilliant!' gasped Jas, doing her 'lost in a desert' act again. 'Water . . . water . . .' she croaked, making the others curl up with laughter.

'We'll come and get the drinks, though,' said thoughtful Mia. 'I expect you've got lots to do, Tom.'

'You can say that again!' he replied. 'What with the party and everything . . .'

The girls' ears pricked up. 'Party?' cried Jas excitedly.

'Yeah. The band's boss, Mr Fortune, has just decided he wants a party for the end of the shoot – here, tonight! You should see the kitchen – canapés and cakes everywhere, and Mrs Bond tearing her hair out!'

'Oh, poor Mum,' said Lauren as the girls got up from their loungers. 'Bang goes her day off.'

Just then, the main door to the pool area opened – the one that currently bore the sign saying RESERVED. The three people who came in ignored the notice. They were talking loudly.

One was an elderly man, white haired and bearded; the others, one man and one woman, were younger and dark haired.

Becky liked the look of the older man immediately. She nudged Mia. 'He's like a sort of slim Father Christmas,' she said.

Tom raised an eyebrow. 'That's the boss himself – Mr Fortune, the managing director of Fortune Records.'

'The big boss?' said Jas. 'The one who wanted the party?' Tom nodded.

Sound carries across water, and it was impossible not to hear what the three people on the other side of the pool were saying – especially as they made no effort to keep their voices down.

'Look, Dad, we've got everything under control,' the younger man snapped. 'You needn't have bothered coming.'

'Oh, come on, Josh,' said the woman, 'you know Dad likes to encourage new talent.'

Mr Fortune nodded. 'Your sister's right. Best bit of the job. There's nothing like the excitement of discovering someone who might be the next big thing . . .'

Lauren, Jas, Becky and Mia exchanged excited looks. 'Tom!' Becky whispered. 'Did you hear that?'

He nodded, looking just a little bit excited himself.

'You've got to give Mr Fortune your CD!' she said.

The record company boss was looking across the room into the spa. He caught sight of the girls and nodded to them, and they smiled shyly back.

'The band's still filming,' Mr Fortune said, turning back to his son and daughter. 'Let's not interrupt now.'

The young woman nodded. 'They should be doing the swimming pool scene shortly, though. Let's meet back here in ten minutes – we can talk to them before they begin that. Come on, Josh.'

She and the younger man left, followed after a moment by their white-bearded father.

Jas grabbed hold of a potted palm, pretending her legs had gone all wobbly. 'Swimming pool scene!' she hissed.

'Ooh yes!' agreed Becky, just as thrilled, and Mia grinned too.

Lauren laughed. 'You three stay here,' she said. 'I'll fetch the drinks.'

Leaving her friends giggling excitedly, Lauren headed off with Tom. The two of them made their way to the bar area, just past the hotel's main reception.

'So,' Lauren said, 'you will give Mr Fortune your CD, won't you, Tom?'

Tom nodded as he went behind the bar. 'Well . . . yes, I guess this is too good a chance to miss.' He began to pour out glasses of the pale yellow lemonade that Lauren knew would have been made that morning from real lemons. 'Those two that Mr Fortune was talking to – they must be Josh and Olivia Fortune, his children. I read on the Internet that they're going to take over when their father retires.'

'Doesn't look like he's thinking of retiring, though, does it?' said Lauren.

Tom agreed. 'I reckon he's still the man in charge.' As he clinked ice into each glass, he took a deep breath and said determinedly, 'I'll try to see him at the party later. If he's on his own, that is. I'll offer him a canapé and then ask if I can give him a copy of my CD.'

'Good one,' said Lauren. She took the tray of drinks from Tom and went back into reception. A short man wearing a tartan waistcoat and glasses was standing in front of the desk. He was saying to one of the receptionists in an American accent, 'Just tell the boys that

Mr Star is here to talk to them. They'll see me.'

'I'll get a message to the band, sir,' the receptionist replied.

The band! He had to mean 4ever! Lauren hurried over to the desk. 'Did you need a message taken to someone, Rosemary?' she said. 'Can I help? You don't want to have to leave the desk, do you?'

Rosemary smiled gratefully. 'Oh, thanks, Lauren, yes please. Could you find 4ever and tell them there's a Mr Star in reception to see them.'

'Sure,' agreed Lauren calmly, but inside she was saying *Yes yes yes yes yes yes yes!*

She was going to talk to the band!

# CHAPTER THREE

Lauren went back to the swimming pool. There were a couple of men putting up large lamps and another pushing a camera into place, but no sign of 4ever. Mia, Becky and Jas were still staring into the spa.

Lauren handed the tray of lemonade to Becky. 'Can't stop,' she said through a very big grin. 'Have to go and talk to the band . . .'

She opened the glass doors, laughing at her friends, who were staring after her with their mouths open. It was pretty enormously exciting that she had a genuine reason to go onto the set. Once into the spa, though, her smile faded and butterflies began to flutter in her stomach.

4ever were busy filming again, so she couldn't interrupt. She watched as blond Pete and dark Jason pretended to be taken by surprise as the other two band-members jumped out from behind a palm tree. All four singers kept collapsing with laughter, and the shot had to be done again and again. Living at the Mayfair Park Hotel, Lauren had met lots of famous people, and sadly not all of them were very nice when they didn't have cameras pointing at them. Seeing 4ever teasing each other and obviously having a lot of fun, she hoped that they were like that the rest of the time too.

Eventually the director, a thin woman with wire-rimmed glasses, announced that she was happy with the shot, and called for a break while she checked preparations at the swimming pool. Lauren took a deep breath and pushed her butterflies aside. She walked confidently over to the nearest boy: red-headed Niall. 'Excuse me,' she said politely, 'there's a Mr Star in reception to see you. All of you,' she clarified.

Niall gave her a smile, and she noticed he had freckles sprinkled over his nose and cheeks, just like her brother Charlie. Of course, in no other way did he resemble her annoying little brother, and she laughed inside for a second at the thought of Charlie as a pop star.

'Hey, lads,' Niall called across to the others, 'come over here.'

The rest of the band turned towards him, and Lauren started to move away, remembering her mum's warning not to bother anyone. But when Niall said, 'Hold on a minute, meet the lads,' she immediately stood still and waited, trying to look professional and calm – but not succeeding in the slightest – as the three boys came over.

'This is—' Niall looked at Lauren and raised an eyebrow.

'Lauren,' she supplied.

'This is Lauren. She says we're wanted in reception.'

'Hey, cheers,' said blond Pete and, to Lauren's amazement, swept into a bow. 'Peter Frost at your service. This is Jason and this is Robin.'

'Seen you around,' said Robin, smiling, which Lauren took to mean that she and the other girls hadn't been quite as discreet as they'd hoped.

She blushed. 'My mum and dad run the hotel,' she said, as a sort of explanation. 'We were told it was OK to watch. We didn't want to get in anyone's way.'

'Nah, you're fine,' said Jason. 'Nice to have a few fans around.'

Niall looked mock-worried. 'We don't know they're fans!'

'Course they are, we're great – aren't we?' Jason said to Lauren, giving her a big grin to show that he wasn't really that big-headed. She nodded eagerly. 'Tell you what,' he continued, 'how's about you show us to reception? Would you mind? I can never find my way around hotels.'

'Sure,' said Lauren happily. 'I expect you stay in loads of hotels, don't you?'

'None as nice as this,' said Niall, and Lauren glowed inside. She was always delighted when anyone praised the Mayfair Park. Of course, it was quite obvious that it was the nicest hotel in the whole country – probably the world – but she still liked it when other people recognized that fact. She'd make sure she told her mum and dad what Niall had said.

Lauren led the band out through the swimming pool area, even though it wasn't the quickest way to reception. She turned her head and mouthed *Oh my God!* as they passed by Jas, Mia and Becky. The girls stared in amazement. This turned to disbelief when Jason gave them a little wave, and the other three 4ever boys smiled across at them. As Lauren and the singers exited, out of the corner of her eye she noticed Jas falling backwards, pretending to faint.

Mr Star was leaning on the desk in reception, but straightened up as the band approached. He opened his arms wide, as though he wanted to give them a hug. 'Boys!' he cried. 'Good to see you!'

Having done her job, Lauren returned to the swimming pool.

'We want to hear everything!' said Becky before Lauren had even sat down.

'Every tiny detail,' Jas insisted. 'Don't miss out *anything*.'

'I can't believe you actually got to talk to the band!' said Mia.

'Yeah, it was OK,' said Lauren, trying to look cool, but she couldn't keep it up. 'It was brilliant!' she cried, and began to tell the others all about it.

'. . . and as I was leaving reception just now, I heard Mr Star say: "Star Music Group could really do with guys like you"!' Lauren finished eventually.

'Star Music Group!' cried Becky. 'Wow!'

'4ever are going to be *sooo* famous,' said Jas excitedly. 'They've got all these record companies queuing up to work with them! And we were there, right at the beginning, seeing them film their first video!'

Only Mia was frowning. 'But if they're working for Mr Fortune and Fortune Records, they can't work with Mr Star too, can they?'

Jas waved a hand, dismissing Mia's concerns.

'Oh, it'll all be fine. Maybe they haven't signed stuff yet or something. Anyway, it's gotta be good, hasn't it? They're in demand! They're gonna be huge! Does it matter who they're working for?'

'But Mr Fortune looked so nice,' said Mia quietly.

At that moment, Mr Fortune himself came into the swimming pool area, followed by his daughter Olivia. The girls stopped talking. Then the director put her head round the door from the spa, and the cameraman gave her a thumbs-up.

'Come on, we'd better get out of the way,' Becky said. 'We shouldn't stay in here while they're filming.'

At that moment, Josh Fortune arrived. He was scowling, and Lauren wondered if he'd spotted 4ever talking to Mr Star and wasn't very happy about it.

'Let's go,' Jas whispered.

They made their way to the spa, found a space by the glass wall and settled down to watch.

The band were now in the swimming pool area. Lauren, Jas, Becky and Mia stared as the four boys took off their brightly coloured shirts, so they were dressed only in swimming trunks. The three Fortunes came over and started talking to 4ever, Josh still looking cross, while a make-up girl hung beautiful flower garlands round each boy's neck.

'Those are called *lei,*' whispered Becky, telling the others that she'd seen them when she'd accompanied her father on a trip to Hawaii – he was a professor of environmental bio-geochemistry and had gone to the islands to examine volcanoes.

'Everyone ready?' called the director as Mr Fortune, Josh and Olivia moved away.

Three of the band-members nodded, but the last one, Robin, appeared to call out to Mr Fortune. The elderly man turned round and, to the girls' astonishment, looked straight at them!

'Oh no,' groaned Jas. 'He's going to tell us to clear out.' Mia looked terrified – she hated getting into trouble.

But the music boss was smiling and nodding. The bewildered girls watched as Robin hurried over to the glass wall and put his head round the door. 'Hey, girls, can't see much from there, can you? Why don't you come a bit closer?' He pointed at four blue-and-white loungers that were placed just by the cameras.

Feeling like she was floating, she was so happy, Lauren led the others through into the pool room. 'Thank you! Thank you!' she said, realizing that even Jas was too overawed to speak to the band or their boss.

'Enjoy yourselves!' called Mr Fortune as he, Josh and Olivia left.

Lauren, Becky, Jas and Mia spent the whole afternoon watching 4ever dancing by the pool and, finally, jumping in with a huge splash. There was a lot of laughter, and Lauren even found herself humming the song again. The best moment came at the very end. The director had called 'That's a wrap!' and the four boys removed the *lei* from around their necks, then came over to where Lauren and her friends were sitting. To their delight, each member of 4ever presented his *lei* to one of the girls, before heading off to get changed.

Lauren knew that she would never want to take off the red *lei* that had been given to her by Niall.

Jas pretended to faint again as she held the orange garland that Jason had placed over her head. 'That was the best day *ever*,' she said, and the others all agreed.

# CHAPTER FOUR

It was only after all the camera equipment had been packed away that the girls realized how long they'd been watching the filming.

'Ooh, I'm so hungry!' said Becky, suddenly noticing that her stomach felt extremely empty. Mrs Bond's famous pancakes seemed a very long time ago, and they'd missed lunch completely.

'Come on, let's go to the kitchen and get something to eat,' Lauren said.

There was a small kitchen, separate from the hotel's huge main kitchen, where food for the café-bar was made, and this was where they found Lauren's mum, surrounded by canapés.

'Girls! Just in time!' Mrs Bond cried as they went in. 'I was about to send Charlie to find you.'

'Could we have a sandwich, Mum?' asked Lauren. 'We're starving!'

Mrs Bond frowned. 'All right, as long as

you're quick,' she said. 'And try not to spill any-thing down your uniforms.'

'Our what?' said Lauren. Her mum pointed to where four dry-cleaner bags were hanging up. Smart black skirts and white blouses could be seen through the clear plastic.

'The main restaurant's fully booked tonight so I need all my waiters there,' Mrs Bond explained. 'And I couldn't get hold of many others at such short notice. So I thought you wouldn't mind helping out – unless you've had enough of 4ever, of course . . .'

'No, no, no!' the girls assured her. They could never have enough of 4ever!

Lauren's mum sighed. 'I shouldn't complain about extra business,' she said, 'but what a day! I've had to whip up most of the food myself because Louis and his team are so busy, and on top of that the biggest dishwasher's packed up!'

It hadn't escaped Becky's notice that Charlie and his best friend Joe were elbow-deep in soapy water, dealing with huge towers of washing-up. Waiting at the party was definitely the better deal!

So after a very hurried and very late lunch, the four girls went into the office next-door and changed into their waitress outfits, before collecting trays of canapés from the kitchen. 'Now, take those into the party, and don't come back till they're empty,' said Lauren's mum sternly.

The girls took their trays downstairs to the ballroom on the basement level, where the wrap party was already underway. They could see Mr Fortune, Olivia and Josh; all the people from the shoot, and lots of important-looking men and women in suits. Pete, Jason, Niall and Robin were there too, of course, now dressed in jeans and T-shirts rather than swimming trunks. The four boys were all busy talking to people in suits, but Niall gave Becky a thumbs-up when he saw her, and took a pastry swirl off her tray.

Tom was there, also handing out canapés.

'Lauren says you're gonna give Mr Fortune your CD,' Becky said as they passed each other. 'Have you done it yet?'

Tom stopped for a moment and patted his jacket pocket. 'No, but I've got it here,' he said. 'Just waiting for a good moment. But he's never on his own.'

'Well, he is the boss,' Becky said. 'Everyone wants to talk to him. I guess you might have to risk it even if there are other people about. Go and offer him some food!'

'That's just it,' said Tom. 'He's not eating anything!'

Becky glanced over at Mr Fortune. He was just waving away a waiter who had offered him a tray of little quail's-egg canapés. 'Oh dear,' she said.

Tom shrugged and moved off to serve other guests. Becky turned to do the same, and found herself face to face with Josh Fortune. He still looked a little bit grumpy, but spoke to her politely. 'Any chance of getting a dessert for the old man?' he said. 'He never touches these savoury bits. Something chocolatey, if you can manage it.'

'Of course,' Becky said, and hurried off to the kitchen. The cakes and desserts were piled on a counter, ready to be taken out later, and she spotted some individual Mississippi Mud Pies, all chocolate and cream. That would do nicely! She took one, remembering to fetch a cake-fork as well, and went back down to the ballroom.

Mr Fortune and Josh were now deep in conversation, and Lauren hovered awkwardly nearby, waiting for an opportunity to hand over the pie. As she was standing there, Olivia Fortune came up. 'Oh, that must be for the old man,' she said – Becky wondered for a moment how *her* dad would feel if she started calling *him* that. 'Thank you so much. You're very kind.' She gave Becky a dazzling smile and took the bowl from her.

Becky went back to the kitchen to get another tray of savoury canapés, thinking that she liked Mr Fortune's daughter a lot better than his son. As she went up the stairs she caught a flash of colour as someone left the kitchen – she thought it looked like a man in a tartan waist-coat. But she had a job to do, and didn't think about it again.

The girls were all enjoying themselves. Jas was having a brilliant time. She loved people and she loved parties, so just being there was fun, even if she was serving food. 4ever's music was playing over the PA system in the ballroom, and Jas thought about her plan to broadcast Tom's CD. It would have worked, she was sure – her plans always did. Well, most of the time, anyway. She looked around to see where Tom was.

Mia came through the door at that moment and paused by Jas. Jas gave her such a hard nudge that she almost dropped her tray! 'Mia, look – Tom's going to give Mr Fortune his CD!' she hissed. The two girls casually walked across the room, trying to look natural and not as though they were trying to get near enough to hear what was being said.

They watched as their waiter friend bravely went up to the record company boss and took a CD out of his pocket. Mr Fortune turned towards Tom, and Jas groaned. 'Bad moment! He's got his mouth full of dessert!'

Olivia was with her father, and she tried to wave Tom away. 'I'm sorry, would you mind letting my father eat in peace?' she said.

'Oh no,' said Jas. Although Olivia had been very polite, Tom was clearly embarrassed and Jas felt sorry for him. But Mr Fortune had swallowed his mouthful of pie, and was now smiling like the jolly Father Christmas Becky had compared him to. 'Thank you, Olivia,' he said, 'but I've had enough anyway. Very kind of you to think of getting this for me, but I'm just not really hungry.' He took the CD from Tom, and handed him his bowl – still with half the Mississippi Mud Pie in it – in exchange. 'I'm sure you won't mind giving a star performance as a waiter – until you're a real star, that is!' he said with a kind laugh, and added something that the girls couldn't hear.

Tom looked delighted as he hurried back towards the door.

'Ooh, I wonder what that last thing was Mr Fortune said,' Jas said. 'Let's go and ask.'

She started to head for the door, but Mia grabbed her arm. 'Mrs Bond told us not to go back up unless our trays were empty,' Mia pointed out.

Jas wrinkled her nose in annoyance, but she was a bit in awe of Lauren's mum and didn't argue. She spotted Lauren and Becky and beckoned them over urgently. Together, Jas and Mia told them about Tom giving his CD to Mr Fortune. The girls were thrilled. 'Oh, Tom's going to be a big star too!' Becky said. 'We'd better get his autograph now!'

'I just want to know exactly what Mr Fortune said to him!' Jas cried. 'I can't bear the mystery any longer!'

'Well, we'd better get rid of this food quickly, then, so we can follow him,' said Lauren with a laugh.

The four girls whirled around the room, pushing their trays under the guests' noses and looking so pleading that nearly every guest found themselves taking a canapé whether they wanted one or not. Jas was getting more and more agitated, and when she saw that the other three had all emptied their platters, she hurriedly shoved her last three blinis in her mouth and raced over to join them. 'I'n reggy,' she said through her mouthful, and the girls burst out laughing. 'I'm ready,' she repeated at last, having finally managed to swallow the food.

But as they turned to leave, a terrible scream rang out.

The girls spun round. It was Olivia Fortune who had screamed. People were rushing over towards her, but it wasn't Olivia they were looking at.

'It's Mr Fortune!' cried Mia. 'He's collapsed!'

# CHAPTER FIVE

There was panic in the ballroom.

Suddenly the door swung open. 'Here comes Mum,' said Lauren in relief. 'She'll sort it all out.'

Mrs Bond was running towards them. She took in everything at a glance. 'Lauren, call an ambulance,' she called. As Lauren hurried off to find a phone – mobiles didn't tend to work down in the ballroom – she heard her mum telling people to clear a space around Mr Fortune, who was still lying on the floor.

There was a phone in a little office by the foot of the stairs. Lauren made the call, calmly and clearly telling the operator that an ambulance was required at the Mayfair Park Hotel. 'We'd better go up to reception to wait for it,' she said to the others, who had joined her. 'The paramedics will need to be shown where to go.'

'Poor Mr Fortune,' said Mia. 'I do hope he's OK.'

'And just as it was all going so well, with him taking Tom's CD and everything,' Jas was saying when there was a huge crash. A platter rolled through the office door and landed at their feet.

The girls looked at each other in surprise, then rushed out to the staircase. To their horror, they found Tom lying halfway down the steps. He was groaning faintly, but his eyes were shut.

Becky took charge. 'Lauren, go and tell your mum what's happened,' she said. 'Mia, go upstairs and wait for the ambulance, and Jas, call 999 again and tell them that someone else has been taken ill at the Mayfair Park. They might have to send another ambulance. I'll stay here with Tom.' She knelt down beside the waiter and the others all ran off. As Lauren headed back to the ballroom, she felt very thankful that Becky was so sensible and organized.

As Mia got to the top of the stairs, Charlie and Joe stuck their heads out of the kitchen. 'What's going on?' Charlie called.

'Can't stop!' Mia shouted back, hurrying on, but the boys weren't going to give up that easily and followed her to reception. Reaching the main doors, Mia told James the doorman that an ambulance would be along shortly, then finally explained to Charlie and Joe what had happened.

'Wow,' said Charlie. 'And we missed it all. What a pain.' They looked a lot more worried about missing the excitement than they were about Mr Fortune or Tom. Mia, who had two brothers, smiled to herself. Typical boys, she thought, knowing they weren't really as callous as they seemed.

After few minutes, Jas joined them, having made her phone call. 'They're sending a second ambulance for Tom,' she said.

Mia took a deep breath. 'Oh, I hope he's all right! Mr Fortune too.' She couldn't bear to think of anyone being ill or hurt. To her relief, the sound of sirens was now approaching. 'At last!' she cried.

Fifteen minutes later, both Mr Fortune and Tom had been carried out on stretchers, and the party guests were beginning to leave.

'What a rotten end to a brilliant day,' said Jas, and Mia had to agree.

The mood was gloomy when the four met at the hotel the next day. 'Any news?' asked Jas as she came into Lauren's room. Lauren shook her head. She'd hung her red *lei* over the end of her bed but even that wasn't making her smile today.

Becky and Mia were sitting on beanbags on the floor. Becky hadn't even made her usual remarks about clearing a path through the mess to get to them.

'The environmental health people are here,' Lauren told the others. 'Mum's all worried that they're going to shut the kitchen.'

'At least it's not the main kitchen,' Mia said. 'You won't have to close the hotel restaurant.'

Lauren shrugged. 'It might not matter if we did,' she said miserably. 'If people think there's something wrong with the food here, they won't come to eat at all. It was in the papers this morning.'

'I saw that,' said Becky. 'It was all about Mr Fortune collapsing, and then in the last bit it just said "a waiter was also affected" or something like that. Poor Tom.'

'I still don't get how anyone could think it was food poisoning,' began Jas. 'Tom's a waiter, he wasn't eating the food.'

'Maybe it was a virus or something,' suggested Mia.

Becky groaned. 'Oh no, I hope not! We might all come down with it.'

'I don't care, as long as no one thinks it's food poisoning,' said Lauren.

The door crashed open and Charlie and Joe fell into the room.

'It's food poisoning!' shouted the boys.

'Charlie! How many times have I told you to knock?!' cried Lauren. 'Or better still, don't come into my room at all.'

But for once, the girls weren't too bothered about Lauren's brother bursting in – it sounded like he and Joe had news.

'Have the environmental health people found something, then?' Mia asked.

'Sort of,' said Joe. 'Guess what? We were the ones with the big, important clue and we didn't even realize it! We saw it all!'

'Saw what?'

Charlie leaped in, anxious to be the one to tell them. 'Tom ate the rest of Mr Fortune's pie! He came into the kitchen and was telling us how he'd been too nervous to eat before the party because of going to give Mr Fortune his CD, but now he was suddenly starving so he took a bite of the pie. Then he got worried 'cos he knew Mum'd be cross, him eating the leftovers, but she wasn't there and we said we wouldn't tell, so he ate the rest of it. Then he went off with another tray of things, and the next thing was, you told us he'd fallen down the stairs.'

The girls were astonished.

'Mr Fortune ate the pie – and a minute later he collapsed,' said Becky. 'And then Tom ate the pie, and a minute later he was ill too.'

'They both ate the same thing,' Joe said. 'So it's got to be food poisoning.'

'Or a nut allergy,' put in Charlie.

'Or a nut allergy,' agreed Joe. 'That makes people collapse.'

'There aren't any nuts in Mum's Mississippi Mud Pie,' Lauren told them, but Joe and Charlie were too carried away to care.

'It only has to be a trace,' said Joe. 'There's a boy like that in our class, and we're not even allowed to take in peanut butter sandwiches for lunch in case we touch him or breathe on him or something.'

'Yes, but it still doesn't seem likely. Not both of them,' said Becky.

Everyone was quiet for a moment, thinking. Charlie and Joe really had provided an important clue, and now the environmental health officers would take away all the rest of the food for analysis. But it looked like the culprit had to be the Mississippi Mud Pie.

'In Science,' said Charlie suddenly, as if his thoughts had been following similar lines, 'we did how one single bac-ter-i-um' – he pronounced it carefully – 'could multiply into millions and millions in only a few hours, if it's in suitable conditions.'

'Conditions like a gooey, creamy, eggy pie!' finished Joe.

'Millions and millions and millions of bacteria,' said Charlie. 'All growing in a pie. And when someone takes a big spoonful . . .'

That was too much for Lauren. 'Out!' she shouted, jumping up and pushing Charlie towards the door. 'Out! Out! Out!'

The boys ran out, laughing.

Lauren wasn't laughing, though. She was suddenly close to tears. 'I didn't believe it could be food poisoning,' she said. 'Mum's so careful. This could ruin the hotel.'

'It won't be that bad,' said Jas. But Lauren couldn't be reassured.

She knew this could be the end for the Mayfair Park Hotel.

# CHAPTER SIX

The next day, the girls went to visit Tom in hospital.

'How are you feeling?' asked Mia.

He gave them a weak smile. 'I'm all right now,' he said. 'Should be going home tomorrow. It's just a mystery what caused it. The doctors are puzzled.'

Lauren screwed up her nose, looking a bit embarrassed. 'Charlie wants me to ask if you have a nut allergy,' she said reluctantly.

Tom laughed. 'Not me. I can eat anything. Although sad to say,' he added, 'it might be a while before I fancy a Mississippi Mud Pie again . . .'

'We're all looking forward to seeing you back at work, Tom,' Mia said.

'Well, until you're a big star, at least!' added Jas.

'I don't reckon that'll be happening any time

soon,' said Tom. 'The nurses told me that Mr Fortune collapsed at the party too. Guess we were both unlucky with the food poisoning or whatever it was.'

'Mum phoned the hospital earlier,' Lauren said, 'and Mr Fortune's getting better too. I'm sure he'll listen to your CD when he's back home again.'

But Tom shook his head. 'He'll have forgotten all about it. And before you say anything' – Jas, who'd obviously been about to protest, shut her mouth – 'I'm not going to remind him. I don't want to get on his nerves.' He smiled. 'Come on, get those miserable looks off your faces! It just wasn't meant to be.'

Jas suddenly remembered something. 'Tom, what was it Mr Fortune said to you, just before you went off with the pie?'

Tom frowned, trying to remember. 'Oh yes,' he said at last. 'He said "break a leg"!'

Jas was shocked. 'He wanted you to break a leg?' she cried.

'No,' said Tom with a laugh. 'He'd been talking about me giving a star performance – and that's just a thing people say before someone goes on stage. It's supposed to bring luck.'

'It didn't bring you much luck,' said Lauren indignantly.

Tom gave her a rueful smile. 'Oh, I don't know,' he said. 'I guess I was just lucky not to *really* break my leg . . .'

'Tom's so nice,' said Becky later as they headed back to the Mayfair Park. 'Isn't it sad that he won't be getting his big chance after all.'

The others agreed.

'This is such a disaster,' said Lauren. 'I wish 4ever had never come to the hotel.'

'You don't mean that!' gasped Jas, who had daily been declaring herself to be the group's biggest fan.

Lauren thought of the red *lei* at the bottom of her bed, and how happy she had felt while they were watching the video shoot. 'Well, OK, not really,' she admitted.

Becky sighed. 'I just wish Josh Fortune had never asked me to bring his dad a dessert . . .'

The time passed really slowly as everyone waited for the environmental health officer's report. By the end of the week the sudden decrease in diners at the Mayfair Park's restaurant seemed to have got a bit too much for Louis

Henri, the hotel's temperamental French chef. He got quite hysterical at the idea that anyone might think there could be food poisoning in a place where he worked – even though, as he himself hadn't even set foot in the small kitchen on the day in question, he couldn't possibly be considered responsible for it. The girls – summoned to the main kitchen by Charlie, who had gone to investigate the noise – arrived just in time to see him throw a trifle at Mr Bond. Luckily no one was hurt, and Mr Bond, who liked Louis very much, saw the funny side of it.

'You look good enough to eat, Dad,' said Charlie cheekily as Mr Bond came out of the kitchen, pink pudding dripping from his grey suit. A stream of apologies followed after him from Louis Henri.

'Are you all right, Mr Bond?' Becky asked.

Mr Bond grinned. 'Nothing could upset me today,' he said. 'And if Louis had let me get a word in before he started lobbing desserts around, I could have told him that he had no need to worry . . .'

'You mean . . . ?' Lauren began, her face lighting up as she guessed what he had to say.

'Yes. The report's back – and everything's fine! Every test was negative.'

'So there was nothing wrong with the Mississippi Mud Pies after all?' Jas asked.

'Every sample was OK,' Mr Bond told them. 'The only thing they couldn't check was the particular pie that Mr Fortune and Tom ate, of course.'

It had been revealed that not only had Tom finished the pie, but either Charlie or Joe (both claimed to be the one who did it) had washed up the plate so not even a crumb remained.

Mr Bond went off to get changed, and Charlie followed him.

'I think that news calls for a celebration!' said Jas.

'Anyone for trifle?' suggested Becky with a smile. 'Or a perfectly-all-right Mississippi Mud Pie?'

'Milkshakes all round in the café-bar, I think,' said Lauren. She was smiling too. As much as her parents had tried to hide it, she knew they'd been really anxious about the suggestion of food poisoning in the hotel. It was a huge relief to know they didn't have to worry any more.

A bit later the girls were sitting in the cosiest corner of the hotel's café-bar, sipping their milk-shakes – two chocolate, one strawberry, one banana. 'What are we going to do today, then?' Jas said.

'We could take Tumble for a walk,' Mia suggested. 'His leg's so much better now, and he gets all restless being at the shelter. He really needs a proper home—'

She was cut off by a gasp from Becky, who had picked up a newspaper that someone had left on the table in front of them and was staring at it in amazement. She held it up so the others could read the headline: UN-FORTUNE-ATE. Underneath was a picture of an elderly, white-bearded man they all recognized. 'It's Mr Fortune,' Becky said. 'He's in hospital – again!'

Lauren, Mia and Jas were all unhappy to hear that Mr Fortune was back in hospital. They listened as Becky read out the story. It explained how Mr Fortune was a car enthusiast, and that he'd received a Jaguar E-Type – 'That's a really cool car,' said Mia – as a birthday present. But the brakes had failed the first time he'd taken it out, and the car had crashed into some railings, leaving Mr Fortune with injuries to his leg as well as cuts and bruises. '*"We're just grateful that Dad's OK, and that no one else was hurt," said Mr Fortune's daughter, Olivia, yesterday. Ms Fortune and her brother Josh are hotly tipped to take over Fortune*

*Records on their father's retirement – but with the boss in hospital yet again, they're getting an early taste of power!'* Becky finished.

'Wow,' said Jas. 'Mr Fortune must be the unluckiest person in the whole world!'

'It's terrible,' said Mia. 'He is SO accident-prone.'

Lauren jumped to her feet. Her eyes were shining with excitement. 'That's not it at all!' she cried. 'Someone must be trying to do him in!'

Mia, Becky and Jas looked at her in astonishment. 'I don't even know what that *means*,' said Jas after a second.

Becky gave a heavy sigh and turned to Jas. 'You know that Lauren's been reading all those detective books?' she said. 'Well, she thinks someone's deliberately trying to hurt Mr Fortune.'

'Oh no!' cried Mia, horrified.

But Jas and Becky were laughing now. 'I saw Charlie doing his spy act behind one of the potted palms earlier,' said Becky. 'Why don't you borrow his magnifying glass?'

Jas held out her hands. 'Do you want to take my fingerprints?' she said.

Even Mia had started laughing.

Lauren wasn't upset by their teasing. Solving

the Case of the Ruby Necklace had made her really interested in detective work, and she'd been reading loads of stories about boys and girls who solved crimes, as well as ones about grown-up detectives and police.

'I'm just looking at the evidence,' she told the others. 'Only Mr Fortune and Tom were taken ill at the party. It has to be the pie that made them sick. But all the other food was OK. That's really suspicious.'

'What do you mean?' asked Jas.

'I mean,' said Lauren, 'that someone did something to that pie. Someone put poison in it. And now someone's cut the brakes on Mr Fortune's car!'

Mia and Jas almost looked convinced. But Becky was frowning as she held up the newspaper again. 'This doesn't say the brakes were cut, just that they failed. And no one even knew Mr Fortune was going to have a Mississippi Mud Pie, did they?'

'Well, Josh did,' said Lauren. 'He was the one who asked you to get a dessert.'

'He couldn't have known which dessert I was going to get, though,' Becky pointed out.

Lauren had to admit she was probably right. 'I suppose it is a bit unlikely,' she said reluctantly.

'Well, I'm pleased,' said Mia. 'It means that no one's trying to hurt Mr Fortune.'

But Lauren couldn't help feeling a bit disappointed. It wasn't that she wanted Mr Fortune to get hurt, of course she didn't. But she had been hoping that they would get to be detectives again, like the people in her books. And although the others were right, and it didn't seem possible that anyone could have known Mr Fortune was going to eat the pie, somehow she couldn't help feeling that there was more to it than just bad luck . . .

# CHAPTER SEVEN

Becky went to fetch another round of milkshakes and when she got back she found the others were talking about Mr Fortune's car crash. Had it really been an accident?

'I've got a plan,' Jas said, after downing almost half her shake in one gulp. 'The paper says which hospital Mr Fortune's in, doesn't it?' Becky nodded. 'So,' Jas continued, 'why don't we go and visit him, before we pick up Tumble? We can ask him questions, like detectives would, and make absolutely sure there's nothing dodgy going on.'

Becky agreed. She thought it was really unlikely that anyone was trying to 'do in' Mr Fortune, as Lauren had put it, but she had been brought up by a scientist who'd taught her always to check the evidence.

'Let's take him some chocolate,' Mia suggested. 'It looks like he's got a really sweet tooth.'

Lauren finished her drink, and then ran off to tell her mum where they were going. Everyone was happy for the girls to spend most of their holidays at the Mayfair Park Hotel, especially Jas, whose mum worked really long hours, but it was agreed that they wouldn't go anywhere else without letting Mr or Mrs Bond know, and they had to always carry their mobiles – although they did that anyway.

Mia's dad had a day off, so she said she'd ask him to give them a lift to the hospital. Luckily, he agreed, and said he would be with them in twenty minutes.

There was just time to go to the shops before Mr Lopez came for them. Lauren's mum had given them some money towards Mr Fortune's gift, so they were able to get a really nice box of chocolates. All four girls were just a bit excited. Could this be the start of another mystery?

It was the middle of visiting time when they arrived at the hospital. Mr Fortune was in a private room, and Becky felt a bit nervous as she knocked on the door. What if Josh and Olivia were there? They might not want strangers crowding round their father. But when a voice called out 'Come in' and they entered, they found that Mr Fortune was alone. He was wearing bright red pyjamas that made him look more like Father Christmas than ever, and his smile was just as jolly as Santa's, although he seemed rather frail and had a bruise on his forehead.

'Hello!' he said. 'Now, don't tell me – I never forget a face. The young ladies from the Mayfair Park Hotel, isn't it?'

They nodded, and Becky introduced them all.

'Well, this is a pleasant surprise,' said Mr Fortune. He frowned slightly. 'It's funny, but now I'm speaking to you, you seem even more familiar. But I'm fairly sure we hadn't met before that day at the hotel, had we?'

The girls looked at each other. After a moment, Becky said, a bit sheepishly, 'We were on the news last term. And in the papers. There was this ruby necklace . . .'

'Of course!' the record boss cried. 'I read all about it! And you girls turned detective and solved the crime, didn't you?'

They agreed, trying to look modest – but the fact was, they were all really proud of their work on the case.

Mr Fortune gave a rueful laugh. 'I could do with some detectives myself. The amount of things that have happened to me lately, I'm almost beginning to think that I'm cursed!'

'What, really?' said Jas, her eyes open wide. She loved anything spooky, and had even been known to miss a party so she could stay at home to watch *Mostly Ghostly* on TV.

Becky didn't believe in curses or ghosts or anything like that, but still wanted to know the details – this could be a clue! 'What sort of things d'you mean, Mr Fortune?' she asked.

'Yes, please tell us!' echoed Lauren and Mia.

Mr Fortune looked a bit surprised that they were so interested, but invited the girls to sit down. They drew chairs up to the bed, Mia and Jas on one side and Becky and Lauren on the other. There was a huge bouquet of flowers on the bedside table next to Becky – an expensive-looking arrangement of lilies and roses, tied up with silver ribbon – and she could read the card propped beside the vase: *With all my love, Olivia*.

Mia produced the box of chocolates. 'We brought you these,' she said shyly.

'We know you like chocolate,' Jas added.

Mr Fortune looked delighted. 'Oh, how kind. How very kind. I am more touched than I can say. But I wonder – would you think me very rude if I opened the box and asked you young ladies to eat them up for me instead? Sadly, recent events have put me off my beloved chocolate for the time being.'

Becky remembered how Tom had said he didn't fancy eating Mississippi Mud Pie again. 'Is that because of the pie at the party?' she asked. 'Oh, thank you,' she added as Mr Fortune offered the box of chocolates and she helped herself to a strawberry cream.

The old man waited until Lauren, Mia and Jas had chocolates, too, before he answered the question. He settled himself back on his pillows and began to speak as though he were telling them a story. 'It's not just the pie,' he said. 'A few weeks ago, I went into my office and found a parcel on my desk, with the rest of my post. I opened it and found a small box of luxury chocolates inside, supposedly a promotional gift. As I am – if you will excuse me blowing my own trumpet – quite an important man in the music industry, I get rather a lot of such things. People send me chocolates, bottles of champagne, tickets to shows, all sorts of gifts that they hope will persuade me to work with them.'

Becky immediately thought how much she'd

like a job in the music business. Not only did you get to meet bands like 4ever, but also people sent you presents when it wasn't even your birthday!

'Now, my particular favourite has always been the cherry fondant,' Mr Fortune continued. 'There were two in the box, and feeling rather greedy, I'm afraid I ate both of them. About half an hour later, I was terribly sick.'

The girls gasped.

'Did anyone else eat any of the chocolates?' Lauren asked.

Mr Fortune looked impressed. 'I can see you're a detective,' he said. 'No, they didn't. Luckily I had been alone when I received the chocolates and indulged myself – and by the time I was well again, the box had disappeared.'

Becky thought that definitely sounded suspicious. Maybe this was a mystery after all! 'Do you know who took the box?' she asked.

Mr Fortune shook his head. 'No, but then I didn't really think much about it. I was just glad to see the back of those chocolates!'

The four girls listened as Mr Fortune continued. He had only just got over being unwell following the chocolate incident when he came to the Mayfair Park. 'I wasn't really hungry,' he told them, 'and I'm not a big fan of those little savoury bites at the best of times. My children thought a dessert might tempt me, but although the Mississippi Mud Pie was delicious, I just couldn't finish it. Strange as it sounds, the box of chocolates that made me so ill may have been a blessing in disguise.'

'What do you mean?' asked Mia.

'I mean, my dear, that I only ate half the pie, because I still had very little appetite following my illness. Had I eaten all of it, I might have been considerably more unwell,' he explained.

Becky frowned. It sounded as though both Mr Fortune and Tom had had a lucky escape.

'And so perhaps you can see,' said Mr Fortune, 'why I am not quite so keen on chocolate as I was – not that I suspect for a second there is any problem with this generous gift of yours,' he added hastily.

Jas, who was on her third caramel cup, looked alarmed for a moment, and the other three girls burst out laughing.

'I came out of hospital following the pie incident, just in time for my birthday. My son Josh presented me with the most magnificent car – classic cars are my hobby, you know – saying it was to cheer me up following my illness, and also to keep me occupied in my retirement.' Mr Fortune suddenly frowned, and told them that he had no intention of retiring just yet, whatever the newspapers might say. 'I just love the music business!' he said. 'D'you know, until all this happened, I'd never even had a day off sick?'

He went on to explain about his accident. He had a driver, but he couldn't resist taking the Jaguar out for the first time himself – and as he went down the long drive at his house, he'd found himself unable to slow down. Scared that he was going to shoot out into the road where he might cause an accident, he deliberately steered into a fence to stop the car.

'That was really brave,' said Becky. She wondered if she would be able to think so quickly in a similar situation – and be courageous enough to risk getting badly injured so no one else would be hurt.

'And so,' said Mr Fortune, 'if it had been just one thing I would have thought I was unlucky. If it had been two things I would have considered myself very unfortunate. But three! You can see why I've begun to wonder what on earth might happen next!'

Becky nodded. Could it really be a

coincidence that Mr Fortune had suffered three 'accidents' in such a short time? It seemed almost unbelievable, but it sounded as if Lauren was right – someone had it in for Mr Fortune. They definitely had a mystery to investigate!

Mia had listened to Mr Fortune's tale in horror. She could hardly believe so many awful things had happened to one person. 'You ought to call the police!' she told him.

The music man smiled gently. 'I don't think the police can stop someone being unlucky, now, can they?' But something about the way he said it made Mia think he suspected it might be more than bad luck – like they did – but he didn't want to believe it.

Jas was obviously thinking along similar lines. She jumped to her feet. 'But someone's got to investigate! It's all so suspicious!'

'Oh yes!' cried Lauren. 'We'll look into it for you. Please let us! You did say you could do with some detectives, and we have solved one mystery already, and it's the summer holidays and we've got nothing to do . . .'

Mia nodded. 'And because we were there

when you got ill at the hotel, it would be natural for us to be interested and ask questions and no one would think it was weird.'

'But my dear young ladies!' exclaimed Mr Fortune, pushing himself up on his pillow. 'I really don't think there's any need . . .'

There was a worried look in his eyes, though, Mia was sure. 'We probably won't find anything,' she said. 'Because there's probably nothing to find.' She took a deep breath, and then said softly, 'And that will put everyone's minds at rest, won't it?'

Mr Fortune darted a sharp look at her, and she knew he understood. He nodded slowly. 'Of course, you're right. There's nothing to discover. But if it would amuse you girls during your holidays . . .'

After a final chocolate from the box, Mia, Becky, Lauren and Jas said their goodbyes and left the hospital room. Jas immediately began to talk about their new case, but Mia nudged her hard in the ribs. Josh Fortune was coming down the corridor towards them.

He obviously recognized the four girls from the Mayfair Park. 'What are you doing here?' he demanded. 'Have you been to see my father?'

'Yes,' said Becky bravely. 'We read about his

accident and came to bring him some chocolates.'

'Chocolates?' Josh looked worried. 'He's stopped eating chocolates. For some reason.'

Jas gave him a hard stare. 'Yes. We know. *And* we know why.'

Mr Fortune's son snorted. 'You shouldn't believe everything the old man tells you,' he said. 'He's getting on. His mind's not as sharp as it used to be.' As the girls left, Mia heard him mutter, 'Sooner he gives up work the better.'

They kept quiet until they were out of the hospital, and then Mia exploded. 'That *awful* man!' she cried. 'How can he talk like that about lovely Mr Fortune!'

Lauren, Becky and Jas stared at her with such surprise that Mia began to laugh. It was true that she very rarely got angry – well, except when people were cruel to animals, of course – and hardly ever said anything nasty about anyone. But Josh had really upset her. She loved her own parents very much, and thought it was terrible that someone could speak like that about their father.

'It's rubbish anyway,' said Becky. 'Mr Fortune's not *really* old. My granddad's older than him, and he does the crossword every day and reads all the new science books and stuff like that. Just 'cos you're "getting on" doesn't mean your mind's not sharp any more.'

Mia had calmed down now, and something else struck her. 'Do you know what's really funny, though?' she said. 'Josh just told us not to believe everything Mr Fortune said. But we know that he was telling the truth, at least about the Mississippi Mud Pie and the car accident.'

Jas jumped in. 'You mean, you think Josh thought his dad might have told us something else? Something he didn't want us to hear?'

Mia nodded. 'I reckon he was worried Mr Fortune might've told us he was in danger.'

'Just like I said!' cried Lauren.

Becky frowned. 'You know what? Josh saying that's convinced me there definitely is something going on.'

'Yeah,' said Jas. 'And we're going to find out what it is!'

Mia's dad arrived to pick them up. 'Could you drop us at the animal shelter, please,' she asked him. 'We want to take Tumble for a walk.'

Tumble's leg was fully healed now, to Mia's relief. It didn't hurt him any more, and he could run about again. But that particular leg would always be a bit weak, the vet at the shelter had told her, which was why Tumble still had a slight limp and seemed to wobble a bit as he ran.

Now he bounded towards them with his funny skipping run when they opened his pen at the shelter, a loveable bundle of brown and grey fur with a furiously wagging tail. He fussed around Mia as she put a lead on him, and then they all went off to the park.

'So, how do we start our investigation?' Becky asked as they walked along by the river.

'We need to make a list of suspects,' Lauren said. 'That's what detectives do. We need to make a list of people who had motive and opportunity.'

'Well, I think Josh Fortune should go right at the top of the list,' said Mia.

Jas suddenly cried, 'Oooh!' The others looked at her. 'Do you remember,' she said, 'when we first saw Mr Fortune and Josh, by the swimming pool? He was all cross at his dad for coming to the shoot. He didn't want him around at all.'

'You're right,' said Lauren, her eyes lighting up. 'And who asked Becky to get Mr Fortune a dessert – Josh!'

'The Jaguar E-Type was a present from Josh,' Mia added. 'But what about the chocolates that made Mr Fortune sick?'

'Well, that's the easiest one of all!' Becky told her. 'Josh works in the same office as his dad, he could have just put the parcel on his desk, then thrown the box away later!'

They all thought about this while Tumble ran around chasing some ducks. After a moment Becky said, 'The thing is – would anyone really do all that to their own father? I mean, I have rows with Dad and stuff, but to cut brakes on someone's car or put poison in their food . . .'

'So what if it's not Josh?' said Lauren. 'Who else can we put on our list of suspects?'

'I know,' said Jas. 'There was that other record company man, the one who came to see 4ever.'

'Mr Star,' Mia said.

'Oh yes!' said Lauren. 'We did wonder how the band could work for him if they were already working for Mr Fortune – and if there was no Mr Fortune, Mr Star with his fancy waistcoats could take all of Fortune Records's clients!'

Mia frowned. She still thought that Josh was the guilty party.

Suddenly Becky gasped.

'What is it?' asked Lauren.

'Does Mr Star wear a *tartan* waistcoat?'

Lauren nodded, bemused.

'I saw him!' Becky cried. 'During the party, just after I got the pie for Mr Fortune. I saw Mr Star – and he was *coming out of the kitchen*!'

# CHAPTER NINE

Lauren, Jas and Mia stared at Becky in astonishment.

'Are you sure?' Mia asked. 'Did you really see Mr Star coming out of the kitchen during the party?'

'Well, I saw the back of someone in a tartan waistcoat, and Lauren says that's what Mr Star was wearing,' Becky told her.

'You didn't see his face, though,' said Jas.

Lauren produced her phone. 'I know someone who might've.'

A minute later she clicked off the phone. 'Charlie says a man did look into the kitchen during the party,' she said. 'He was short, with a tartan waistcoat and glasses, and had an American accent. He just said, "Sorry, wrong room." Charlie didn't see him go near the food, but he was too busy washing up to pay much attention.' She looked triumphant. 'His description totally fits Mr Star!'

Jas's eyes were shining. 'Then we've solved it! We've solved the mystery!'

But Becky shook her head. 'I know it's really suspicious, but we need more evidence than that.'

Mia had got out her mobile phone and was busy using it to access the Internet, while Lauren started to tick off the various incidents Mr Fortune had told them about. 'One, the poisoned chocolates,' she said. 'Well, Mr Star would know where Mr Fortune's office is, wouldn't he? And he'd know the sort of thing a music boss would get in the post, promotional gifts and stuff, because he's one too. Two, the Mississippi Mud Pie. We know that he was in the kitchen, and maybe he'd been in the party and overheard Josh ask Becky for a dessert.'

'What about the car?' Jas asked.

'Three, the car,' Lauren continued, nodding at Jas. 'Well, in books, criminals are *always* cutting people's brakes, so I reckon it must be quite an easy thing to do, if you just know a bit about cars.'

'That's what we need to find out, then,' put in Jas. 'If Mr Star knows anything about cars.'

'He has three cars,' said Mia. 'A Rolls-Royce, a Porsche – and a Jaguar.'

The others gaped at her. Laughing, she held up her mobile. 'I just Googled him. And listen to this: Fortune Records has won *four* bidding wars against Star Music Group in the last year.'

'So he's definitely got a motive, then,' said Becky. 'He must really hate Mr Fortune, as well as wanting to get his clients.' She thought for a moment. 'We still don't have any proof, though.'

They found a shady spot beneath a tree and sat down. There was an ice-cream van parked near the river, and it wasn't long before they decided that ice-creams were exactly what they all fancied. Mia and Tumble headed off to the van, and returned after a few minutes with four cones, each with a chocolate Flake stuck in the top. They licked the sweet, swirly ice-cream happily, and for a few minutes no one mentioned Mr Star or record companies or poisoned pies.

Mia began throwing a tennis ball for Tumble with her free hand. The dog was clearly having a wonderful time, and each of the girls was wishing she could take him home, but it wasn't possible. Living in a hotel meant no pets for Lauren, and the same went for Jas, who lived in a flat. Mia's parents had already said that their one dog was enough, and Becky reluctantly decided that it wouldn't be fair to take Tumble to live with her. 'There's only Dad at home,' she said, 'and you know how absent-minded he is. When he gets stuck into his work he forgets about everything else. He'd never remember to feed Tumble or take him for walks, and I'm either at school or at the hotel or doing homework, so I wouldn't really have time to look after him either.' She grinned suddenly. 'I think looking after my dad almost counts as having a pet – I don't think I could cope with another one too!'

Lauren, Jas and Mia laughed, but they knew it wasn't really funny. They all admired Becky for managing to take care of her dad and their home since her mum died, and at one time or another each of them had wondered how she managed to remain so cheerful.

'If it was your dad who'd been poisoned,' Mia said, 'it would probably be because he'd got some experiments mixed up.'

'And I wouldn't be at all surprised!' Becky said. 'I've found him making hot chocolate using a beaker over a Bunsen burner before! But I don't reckon Mr Fortune does that sort of thing.'

They were all quiet for a moment. Mia finally said, 'I keep thinking about how awful it must be to believe someone wants to hurt you. We have to find out the truth.'

'I've got a plan for that!' Jas burst out. Becky, Lauren and Mia looked at her expectantly. 'We go to the Star Music Group building and look for evidence there! If we search Mr Star's office we're bound to find something.'

'I read a book where the detective found arsenic behind a secret panel in someone's office,' put in Lauren.

Becky was frowning slightly. 'It's a good idea,' she said, 'but how are we going to get into Mr Star's office?'

Mia suddenly gasped. 'I've just noticed the time!' she said. 'I have to get Tumble back to the shelter.'

Lauren looked down at her wrist. 'Oh no!' she said. 'My watch must've fallen off! The strap was a bit loose earlier. What a pain.'

Mia hurried off, but the others spent the next ten minutes searching for Lauren's watch – without any luck. In the end, Lauren decided to give up. 'I really need to get home. Mum'll be waiting for me. Got chores to do, you know.'

'But you can't go – we've got to work out how we're going to get into Star Music Group!' said Jas.

In the end they decided that Jas would go home with Becky, and the two of them would come up with a plan. With any luck, they'd be able to do it the very next day.

For the second time that holiday, Lauren found herself being woken by her mum, way before she was ready to get up. She would happily stay in bed all morning if she could, snoozing or day-dreaming or perhaps reading one of her detective books.

Today was – or had been – a snoozing sort of day. Vaguely aware of hearing her mum say that her friends were waiting in the kitchen, Lauren turned over and went back to sleep, plunging herself into a weird dream in which a man in a tartan waistcoat was mixing poisoned drinks over a Bunsen burner in the hotel bar.

'Wake up, Lauren! Wake up!' She was torn from her dream by Jas's voice, and reluctantly opened her eyes. Jas, Mia and Becky were all perched on the side of her bed, Becky nibbling on a slice of toast.

Lauren sleepily dragged herself up onto her elbows.

'Come on, you've got to get up,' Jas said. 'Today's the day we solve the mystery!'

'Jas and I worked out what to do,' added Becky. 'And you're part of it, of course.'

Becky and Jas explained their plan. They had decided that they needed two things – a reason to be at the Star Music Group building in the first place, and a distraction to allow them to get into Mr Star's office without being noticed. Lauren and Mia were going to provide both of them! They would pretend to be a girl band who wanted Mr Star to sign them up to his music label. That would explain their visit. Then they would have to put on a performance for the receptionist, so he or she wouldn't notice Becky and Jas sneaking past.

It was at this point that Lauren found herself fully awake, and she started protesting loudly. Mia, who was obviously hearing the plan for the first time too, seemed just as unhappy.

'You know I can't sing!' Lauren cried. 'I can't even do "Happy Birthday"!'

Becky rolled her eyes. 'What does that matter? You watch the telly! Most of the people who want to be in bands can't sing. It'll probably make it more convincing!'

'I couldn't do it!' Mia looked terrified. 'I couldn't sing in front of *people*!'

In the end, Lauren gave in and agreed to sing

– or at least try – but Mia couldn't be budged. Knowing how shy their friend was, the others didn't keep trying to persuade her. Jas said she'd swap places and be part of the girl band instead, and Becky agreed that that was actually a better plan, because Mia was the computer expert, the one who'd be able to access Mr Star's records – find out if he'd been looking up poisons, or how to fix a Jaguar, stuff like that.

'There's only one problem with the new plan,' said Jas.

'What's that?' Lauren asked.

'Well,' Jas said, 'now that I'm part of the band, they're probably going to want to sign us.' She sighed theatrically. 'And I don't know how I'll deal with all the fame and fortune . . .!'

# CHAPTER TEN

Lauren got up and changed out of her nightshirt. She really wasn't keen on dressing up or wearing make-up, but Becky and Jas persuaded her that she had to look like she really was in a girl band. Becky went through Lauren's wardrobe to try to find something she considered suitable. In the end, she chose a short black skirt and a black T-shirt with a sequinned butterfly on it. 'And you can wear your Christian Lees,' she added, referring to the designer shoes that Lauren had been given as a reward when they solved the Case of the Ruby Necklace.

Although Lauren wasn't interested in clothes, putting on the beautiful red ballet flats with their black satin bows always made her smile. They gave her a kind of confidence, the idea that passersby would glance at her feet and gasp in amazement at how stunning her shoes were, then look up and realize with astonishment that the sophisticated woman wearing them was actually a schoolgirl!

As she slipped on the shoes, Lauren could almost – although not quite – understand why some people got so excited about designer gear.

She borrowed lip-gloss and mascara from Jas – who, even in her everyday clothes of denim shorts and a white T-shirt with a strawberry on it, looked like she could be in a girl band – and some blusher from Becky. Jas borrowed a couple of scrunchies from Mia and pulled her shoulder-length black hair into bunches.

The two posed together, grabbing a hairbrush each from Lauren's dressing table and staring into an imaginary camera. 'How do we look?' Lauren asked, laughing.

'Wow,' said Mia.

But Becky was frowning slightly. 'It's not quite right,' she said. 'Oh, you look great. But you don't look like a band, not just the two of you. You need another member.'

Mia looked scared. 'Oh Becky, I can't . . .' she began.

Becky reassured her with a smile. 'No, we'll need both of us in the office,' she said. Then, after a moment's thought, 'What about Charlie?'

'Charlie?' cried Lauren. What an idea! Her

pain of a little brother being part of their plan – that was just ridiculous!

But Becky talked down Lauren's protests. Charlie, she pointed out, might be a prize pain, but he was also very lively and *distracting* – and a distraction was exactly what they were after.

'And he can be kind of cute,' added Mia. 'You know all the guests in the hotel love him.'

'Yeah, remember when he dressed up in that evening suit with the bow tie and kept opening doors for people?' said Jas. 'Didn't some American woman say he was "darling" and try to give him a fifty-dollar tip?'

'Yes,' said Lauren, 'but Mum wouldn't let him take it. Anyway, he was only dressed like that because he was pretending to be James Bond. Again.'

'But the point is, he can be really charming. And isn't he in the school choir too?' Becky said. 'So he can sing, at least.'

So they went to find Charlie. He was in the kitchen of the Bonds' flat, alone as both Mr and Mrs Bond were now at work in the hotel. He burst out laughing when he saw Lauren. 'You look like a Barbie doll!' he said, sniggering and pointing at her made-up face.

Lauren was on the point of turning round and

leaving, but then she thought of Mr Fortune lying in his hospital bed and realized they had to do whatever they could to solve the mystery, even if it involved putting up with her pesky brother. She let Becky explain that they wanted his help.

At first, though, Charlie wasn't interested in taking part in any 'girlie' plan, as he called it. It was actually Mia who came up with the idea of referring to it as a secret mission, which made Charlie's ears prick up, and when he learned that he would be expected to sing, dance, and generally be the centre of attention, *and* there might be an ice-cream in it for him, he finally agreed.

Just before they left the flat, Lauren popped back into her room to grab a pair of sunglasses and a baseball cap. 'For the pop-star look?' Becky said.

'No,' Lauren replied. 'Remember how bad my singing is? I don't want anyone to recognize me!'

They found Mrs Bond and told her they were all going out – although they left out most of the details. Lauren's mum was pretty cool, but she might not react well to learning they were planning to sneak into someone's office, even if it was for a really good cause.

* * *

On the way to the offices, they sat on the bus and tried to come up with a name for their band. 'They'll expect us to have one,' said Charlie, acting as if the whole thing had been his idea all along. 'We need it for very-silly-me-tude.'

'Verisimilitude,' corrected Becky.

'Bet you don't even know what that means,' added Lauren.

'Course I do,' Charlie said smugly. 'It means making something look true even if it isn't. You know I'm top in English. I got ten out of ten in spelling last week and *two* gold stars on my story—'

'Yeah, yeah.' Lauren hastily cut off her brother's boasting, especially as she hadn't been entirely sure what 'verisimilitude' meant herself. 'I thought we were thinking up band names.'

After rejecting most of Charlie's names, they finally settled on 'Charlie and the Angels'. He said the idea came from an old TV programme about private eyes. Lauren wasn't keen, because it made Charlie seem like the most important one, but by that time the bus had reached their stop and there wasn't time to think of any others. Anyway, even though she wasn't going to admit it, she was actually getting just a little bit excited at the thought of the adventure that lay ahead, so she didn't really mind what name they used.

Jas looked at her watch. 'Just about right,' she said.

'For what?' Lauren asked.

'Duh!' Jas said. 'For lunchtime! We can't go in there when Mr Star's in his office.'

'But what if he has a sandwich at his desk?' said Lauren.

Mia held up her phone. 'Google again,' she said. 'Becky texted me last night and asked me to find out. Mr Star's favourite restaurant is Romana's, and he has lunch there almost every day. His PA books him a table in the morning, and I phoned up to check and there's one booked for today at one-thirty. He should be on his way any time now.'

The bus stop was almost opposite the Star Music Group offices, so they sat on the bench there to watch the main doors. Becky made Lauren hold a magazine in front of her face. 'You're the only one of us he's seen before, 'cos Charlie says he didn't look at him and I only saw the back of him so he couldn't have seen me,' she said.

'Yeah, well, he hardly looked at me either,' said Lauren and pointed out that she was now wearing a cap and sunglasses anyway, but Becky insisted. She was a great believer in doing things thoroughly. There was no point in risking something if a little bit of effort might make all the difference, and any scheme she came up with was always planned down to the tiniest detail.

They'd only been waiting on the bench for a few minutes when a short man in a flowery maroon waistcoat came out of the doors. 'Is that him?' Jas asked Lauren.

Lauren peeped over the top of her magazine. 'Uh-huh,' she said. 'He's wearing a different waistcoat today, but that's definitely Mr Star.'

They gave him a few minutes to get out of sight, and then hurried over the road.

Becky told Jas, Lauren and Charlie to go in first. She and Mia hung around just outside the doors, watching, listening and waiting.

Inside the foyer, a receptionist was busy eating her lunch at the front desk.

'Hello,' said Jas with a big smile on her face. 'Is this Star Music Group?' When the receptionist nodded, Jas cried out: 'Then it's your lucky day! We present the next big thing . . .' She stood back and threw out her arms as Charlie came forward to yell:

'It's . . . Charlie and the Angels!'

The three of them started to jump around in the foyer, Charlie and Jas singing the latest Number One at the top of their voices, while Lauren did a sort of quiet 'la la la', but made up for it by joining in with the very energetic dancing. Charlie began drumming along the edge of the receptionist's desk, then jumped up on it to drum on her desk lamp, in-tray and telephone.

While the receptionist was distracted – and she was definitely distracted by that! – Lauren beckoned to Becky and Mia. They opened the door quietly, and crept through the foyer and down a short corridor. At the end of it was a staircase, which they scampered up. Even when they reached the top, they could still hear 'Charlie and the Angels', who were now onto the second verse. It was very hard not to giggle, but Becky knew they mustn't risk making a noise and attracting attention.

At the top of the stairs, Becky nudged Mia. A sign on the wall pointed to, in one direction, the toilets, and in the other direction the managing director's office. Her plan was proceeding perfectly! From where they stood, it looked like the door to Mr Star's office was open, and they crept towards it. But when they arrived, Becky got a shock. The door led into a sort of anteroom – an outer office with another door on the far side. In this outer office was a desk, and behind the desk sat a woman.

There was no way they could reach Mr Star's office without being seen.

# CHAPTER ELEVEN

'Oh no!' whispered Mia as she peered round the corner of the door. So near and yet so far! Somehow they had to cross the outer office – but they couldn't possibly do it without the woman seeing them. She was looking down at her desk, reading a magazine, but she would definitely notice if anyone entered the room. 'That's Mr Star's PA,' she whispered to Becky. 'Her photo was on the Star Group website. Her name's Marigold Something-or-other.'

But Becky was still staring into the office. 'Look at her shoes,' she whispered. 'They've just got to be designer.'

Mia carefully put her head round the door, but gave a shrug. She liked fashion, but wasn't as madly interested as Becky, who had really started to study it since their encounter with the famous actress Isabella Duval. Anyway, even if the PA's shoes were a designer brand, why was that important?

'Her handbag's designer as well – and look, there's her mobile phone sticking out of it. That's perfect,' Becky continued. It was clear to Mia that her friend had a plan – but she couldn't think what it could possibly be.

At that moment, Marigold the PA got up and walked over to the far side of the room, where there was a sort of mini kitchen with a kettle and some mugs. Mia's eyes widened in horror as Becky suddenly fell to her knees and began to crawl as quickly as she could towards the woman's desk. Mia had to clap a hand over her own mouth to stop herself from gasping out loud.

A few seconds later, though, Becky was back by her side, and dragging Mia towards the loos. They dived into the ladies, where Becky proudly displayed a mobile phone.

'Oh no!' Mia cried, horrified. 'Becky, we'll get into such trouble! That's stealing!'

Becky looked a bit embarrassed, but said, 'No it's not, it's just borrowing. I just want to get her number, then I'll put it back. Anyway, we're detectives, aren't we? Sometimes we just have to do stuff like that.'

Mia agreed, although she still had a bit of a

sick feeling inside, the sort she always got when she was worried. But she knew they had to get to the bottom of the mystery.

Becky was pressing buttons on the phone, accessing the contacts list. 'Bother,' she said after a few moments. 'There's no "my number" entry like there is on my mobile. What do we do now?'

'Oh, that's easy,' said Mia. 'Just call me and the number will come up on my phone.'

'Anyone ever told you you're a genius?' Becky said, grinning. She quickly keyed in Mia's mobile number, and a second later Mia's phone began to ring. Mia hurriedly rejected the call, just in case anyone could hear the ringtone from outside the toilets – although they probably wouldn't hear anything above the sound of Charlie and the Angels, still going strong downstairs.

'Stay here,' whispered Becky, and she slipped out of the ladies. Mia held her breath – they'd been very lucky so far, but what if Becky got caught? But there was no need to worry. Becky returned in less than a minute. 'I've put her phone back – she was still busy making coffee,' she told Mia. 'Now, text her something like this . . .' She paused for a moment. 'All right, I've got it. Begin "Hi Marigold", then it'll look like it's from someone who knows her.'

Mia began keying in the words.

'Then say . . . "Huge sale at your fave shop, one day only, everything going fast, get here now", and put lots of exclamation marks. Then say . . .' She stopped, looking astonished. 'My mind's gone blank. Name me a designer!'

Mia laughed. 'How about – Christian Lee!' she said.

Becky rolled her eyes towards the ceiling. 'I'm such an idiot! OK, then add, "I'll save you a pair of Christian Lees but you'd better hurry." Don't sign it just send it. She'll think it's from one of her mates who's got a new phone or something.'

There was a *beep* as the text whizzed off on its way. The two girls peered out into the corridor, and heard a faint double beep as it arrived at its destination. Becky gave Mia a thumbs-up.

An excited squeal came from the PA's office. A minute later, Marigold herself came down the corridor, jogging as fast as she could on five-inch heels. She headed down the stairs, and Mia gave a sigh of relief. It had worked!

'Come on,' Becky said. 'This is our chance!'

Even though they knew the office was empty, they still crept down the corridor as quietly as they could. They crossed the PA's room to the door labelled MANAGING DIRECTOR. Luckily, the door wasn't locked.

'How long d'you reckon we've got?' Mia said nervously.

'Well,' said Becky, 'I'd say at least half an hour before Mr Star or his PA get back – but about five minutes before Lauren totally freaks out at having to keep singing for so long!'

Mia laughed. 'We'd better hurry up, then!' She forgot all her nervous feelings as she sat down at Mr Star's desk, which held a monitor, keyboard and printer. This was where she felt totally at home, in front of a computer.

Becky began searching the room, and Mia could hear the 'tap tap tap' as her friend looked for secret openings – that had been Lauren's idea. But, 'Nothing,' Becky called disappointedly after a few minutes.

'Have you looked at the bookshelves?' Mia asked, not taking her eyes off the computer screen. 'To see if there are any books about poison or cars?'

There was a pause, then Becky said with a sigh, 'Nothing. It's all pop music and bands.'

'Same here,' said Mia. 'I can't see anything suspicious at all.'

'I don't think we're going to find anything,' said Becky. 'He must have got rid of the evidence, or hidden it somewhere else. I guess we'll have to try to find out where he lives. But I don't know how we'll get into his house. Maybe—'

But Mia was staring at the screen. She'd suddenly had an idea – and it had worked! 'Becky! Look at this!' she cried.

Becky hurried over to the desk. 'You've found something? Evidence?'

'Yes – evidence that Mr Star is innocent!' Mia explained how she'd searched for files containing the word 'Fortune' and discovered a letter that Mr Star had written to the Fortune Records boss. In it, Mr Star suggested teaming up for a joint venture called 'Star Fortunes'. He said how much he admired Mr Fortune – he called him 'Samuel' – and bore no grudges about being beaten in the recent bidding wars, but thought it would bring rewards for both of them if, instead of competing, they worked together.

'And look at the date on the letter,' Mia said. 'It was written the day after Mr Fortune's car accident – before anyone would have heard about it. You wouldn't try to put someone in hospital one day, and then offer to work with them the next!'

'You might if you were really sneaky,' said Becky.

Mia shook her head. 'Anyway, I don't believe anyone would try to do something as terrible as that just to steal a few of someone else's clients. Mr Star will be able to work with all of them if the two firms merge!'

She hit *print* to get a hard copy of the letter, then closed down the file and emptied History, so there was no evidence of her searches.

Meeting no one – luckily – they left the room and went back down the stairs to the foyer. To their utter astonishment, Lauren was now using the receptionist's stapler as a microphone, and singing at top volume. Unable to help themselves, they burst out laughing. Lauren hadn't been exaggerating when she said she was no singer! The poor receptionist was trying to get rid of Charlie and the Angels but they were ignoring her.

Mia caught Lauren's eye and gave her a thumbs-up, then she and Becky slipped back out through the main doors. As soon as they were outside, Lauren and Jas stopped singing. It took them a few seconds to silence Charlie, who had been thoroughly enjoying himself.

'Thanks for your time,' said Lauren to the astonished receptionist, 'but we can see you're not interested.'

'Yeah, thanks anyway!' Jas called back over her shoulder.

Reunited on the pavement outside, the four girls collapsed into giggles. Charlie watched them pityingly for a few moments, and then said, 'I think someone mentioned ice-cream . . .?'

Mia managed to smother her laughter. 'Come on, we'd better leave before Mr Star gets back,' she said. 'And Lauren, Jas – we have got so much to tell you!'

After a brief stop at a shop for choc ices, the four girls and Charlie caught the bus back to the Mayfair Park, and Lauren made them all cheese and tomato sandwiches in the Bonds' kitchen.

Charlie, who had decided on the way home that a music career would interfere with his spying work, took his sandwiches into the lounge so he could watch television. The girls sat down at the kitchen table to discuss matters.

When they saw the letter about 'Star Fortunes', Jas and Lauren agreed it was unlikely that Mr Star would try to poison someone and then offer to work with him immediately afterwards.

'But Mr Star did go into the kitchen during the party,' said Jas. 'That's still really suspicious.'

Becky suddenly thumped the table. 'I'm an idiot!' she cried. The others stared at her, and she explained, 'I saw Mr Star coming out of the kitchen *after* I'd taken the pie to Mr Fortune! Charlie and Joe said he only popped in for a moment – he couldn't possibly have poisoned the pie before I took it!'

Lauren gaped at her. They were *all* idiots! How had they not spotted that before?

So they all agreed that, even if Mr Star's innocence wasn't *completely* proved, he was at least now at the very bottom of their list of suspects.

'Which means Josh's jumped to the top again,' Mia pointed out.

'I know what we should do next,' said Becky. 'We haven't been able to find out yet who gave Mr Fortune the chocolates, or who poisoned the pie. But we could find out more about his car. You know, see who had access to it and could have tampered with the brakes.'

The others thought this was a great idea.

'I've got a plan for that!' said Jas. She explained her idea. They would go to Mr Fortune's house, taking Tumble with them. Then they'd knock on the door and say they'd found a dog wandering about nearby, had he escaped from the house?

'But won't it be Josh or Olivia who answers the door?' said Lauren. 'They'll recognize us and think it's really suspicious.'

Mia held up her phone again. 'Josh and Olivia don't live with their dad,' she said. 'But he has a housekeeper who comes in every day, and a driver, and a man who looks after the garden. So there should be someone there to talk to.' She smiled. 'You can find out almost anything on the Internet if you know how to look.'

'Well, then,' said Jas with a grin, 'let's just look up "Who poisoned Mr Fortune?" – it'd save us a lot of bother!'

When they'd finished their sandwiches, they set off out again. First they visited the animal shelter to collect Tumble – who was delighted to see them – then they caught yet another bus.

Mr Fortune's house had a long drive, as he had told them, with gardens stretching to either side. Mia unclipped Tumble's lead and led him towards the house with a hand through his collar. Two cars were parked near the house, a dark red one and a silver one. As they got closer, the girls could see that the red one was dented and scratched. They reckoned this must be the Jaguar that Mr Fortune had steered into the hedge.

'Wow, what a fab-looking car!' said Lauren.

'Totally glam!' said Becky.

Mia smiled. 'The Jaguar E-Type is generally considered the most beautiful car of all time,' she said. 'Or at least, that's what it says on the Internet.'

It was Jas who knocked at the door. A plump woman with rosy cheeks opened it and smiled at them. They all liked the look of her immediately.

'Excuse me,' said Jas politely, 'but is this your dog?' Mia led Tumble forward. 'We found him just out there' – Jas pointed down the drive – 'and thought he might have got out of the house somehow.'

The woman shook her head. 'No, my ducks, he doesn't belong here, more's the pity.'

'We think he might have been in an accident,' said Mia. 'He's limping.'

On cue, Tumble gave a sad little whine.

'Oh, the poor love!' said the housekeeper. 'I know what, you just bring him along inside for a minute, and I'll get him some water and maybe a little something to eat – and I'm sure you girls could do with a nice cool drink too.'

The girls happily agreed, and followed the woman – her name, she told them, was Gwen – to the kitchen, where she fussed over Tumble and gave him a bowl of water and a few scraps, which he wolfed down eagerly, despite having been fed already at the shelter.

'Mr Fortune – that's the man who lives here, I just look after the house for him – he adores dogs,' Gwen said as she poured them all glasses of orange juice. 'But all he does is work, work, work, there's no time left for a pet.' She suddenly gasped. 'Oh no! He was in a car crash just a few days ago – what if this poor mite was hit? No one saw a dog, but he could have limped away, all hurt and sad . . .'

Mia hastened to reassure her. 'I don't think he's that bad,' she said. 'It looks like whatever happened to his leg has healed now anyway.'

'We'll take him to the vet's,' added Jas. 'They'll make sure he's OK.'

'Was Mr Fortune badly hurt in the car crash?' asked Becky, delighted that Gwen had brought up the subject first. 'We saw that beautiful car in the drive – was that the one he was driving?'

'The red Jaguar, you mean?' said Gwen. 'Yes, that's right. The other one, the silver Mercedes, that belongs to Mr Fortune's son. He was here at the time of the accident and left it behind when he went in the ambulance with his father. He said he'd come back over and collect it when he had the time.'

The girls asked more questions about the

accident. Gwen seemed to find their curiosity perfectly natural, and told them the whole story. They listened carefully, hoping they might pick up some scraps of information, things that Mr Fortune hadn't told them, but they didn't learn anything new.

While Gwen was speaking, the back door opened and a tall man came into the kitchen. She introduced him as Terry, Mr Fortune's driver. 'He's not very busy at the moment, though, what with Mr Fortune being in hospital,' Gwen told them.

Terry helped himself to a glass of juice, and began to make a fuss of Tumble. He appeared happy to answer all the girls' questions, with Gwen chipping in. Both obviously enjoyed gossiping, and didn't seem to notice how nosy their visitors were being!

As far as Terry knew, the Jaguar hadn't left the garage between the time Josh had presented it to Mr Fortune, and the time it had been taken out and crashed. Gwen and Terry both had keys to the garage. So did Josh – who loved dogs and classic cars just as much as his father did, Terry said – even though he didn't live at the house any more. Olivia had a key too. 'Although she's not so interested in cars,' Gwen put in. 'Or dogs, for that matter.' Josh and Olivia were Mr Fortune's only children, and his wife had died when they were young. (Becky felt a sharp pang when Gwen told them that. She knew how awful it was to grow up without a mother.)

Finally they seemed to have got all the information possible, and Becky began to worry that it would seem suspicious if they stayed much longer. After a few meaningful glances at the others, she got to her feet and said they'd better be going if they wanted to get the dog – she nearly said Tumble, forgetting they weren't supposed to know him – to the vet's.

'I'll give you a lift,' said Terry, standing up too.

'No!' shouted all the girls at once, and then realized how rude that sounded. But of course they weren't really going to the vet's, and anyway their parents would go crazy if they accepted a lift from someone they'd only just met, even if he seemed nice. After all, he'd have to go on their list of suspects, thought Becky, although she didn't really think he was the criminal.

'Er, I mean, thank you, but my dad's going to pick us up,' Becky told Terry. 'He'll be happy to take us to the vet's.' She glanced at her watch. 'Hey, we're late meeting him! We'd better go, everyone!'

They almost ran out of the house. 'That was really awkward,' said Mia.

'I was a bit worried that Josh would suddenly arrive to pick up his car,' said Lauren as they passed the silver Mercedes in the drive. 'We really don't want to bump into him again.'

'Oh!' said Mia suddenly. 'Look!' She pointed at the Mercedes' number plate. The last three letters were JAS.

'Wow! How cool is that?' said Jas with a grin. 'Wonder if he'd sell it to me when I'm old enough to drive!'

'Oh, there'll only be electric cars by then – you know, to save the planet,' said Becky.

'Or they'll only allow bikes,' said Lauren.

'Or horses!' Jas added.

'I'd like that,' said Mia thoughtfully. 'I wonder if we've got room for a horse in our garden . . .'

The others laughed. As if Mia didn't already have enough pets!

They caught the bus back to the animal shelter, where they said goodbye to Tumble. Then they returned to the Mayfair Park and, sitting in Lauren's room, began to discuss what they'd learned.

'The Jaguar must've been all right when Mr Fortune first got it,' said Jas, 'otherwise it would've crashed on the way to the house. So whoever tampered with it has to be one of the people who have access to the garage – Mr Fortune, Josh, Olivia, Gwen or Terry.'

But Lauren shook her head. 'Didn't you see?' she said. 'There was a row of hooks just inside the back door, with keys hanging from it. I reckon one of them was a key to the garage. It wouldn't be too difficult for someone to sneak in and take it.'

Becky frowned. That was some good detective work by Lauren, but it just took them back to square one. Anyone could be the guilty party!

'I still think it's Josh,' Jas said. 'It'd be too risky for some stranger to steal a key from Mr Fortune's house, and we know everything else points to him.'

But now it was Mia who was frowning. 'What's up?' Becky asked her. 'I thought you didn't like Josh.'

'I don't,' Mia said. 'It's just . . . well, Terry said that Josh loved dogs, like his dad. And it's hard to imagine someone who loves dogs doing something as awful as this . . .'

'But what Terry actually said was that both Mr Fortune and Josh loved dogs – *and classic cars*,'

Jas reminded her. 'Josh is the one who'd know how to fiddle with the brakes.'

'I suppose so,' said Mia, and Lauren nodded, too.

Becky sighed. It looked like Josh was still at the top of their list of subjects. But how could they ever tell Mr Fortune that they thought *his son* was trying to get him out of the way?

# CHAPTER THIRTEEN

Having decided that Josh was their most likely suspect, the girls sat in silence for a few minutes, thinking. It was Lauren who spoke first.

'We still haven't got any proof,' she said. 'And you know how the Jaguar was a present from Josh? Well, in detective stories, the criminal never does things like that, in case he gets suspected. So if it is Josh, he's being a bit stupid – and I reckon he'll make a big mistake soon, and then we'll get him.'

'You mean he'll try again?' said Mia, worried.

'Uh-huh,' said Becky. 'I'm pretty sure whoever's after Mr Fortune hasn't finished yet.'

'I think we've got to do two things,' said Lauren. 'Number one, find some proof that we can show to Mr Fortune or the police, and number two, stick close to Mr Fortune so if Josh or whoever it is has another go at him, we can jump in and stop it.'

'And I've got a plan!' announced Jas.

The others laughed. That was Jas's catch-phrase!

At that moment, Mr Bond put his head round the door of Lauren's bedroom to say he had to go out, and would any of the girls like a lift home? Seeing to their surprise that it was teatime already – they'd done so much that day that the time had whizzed by! – Mia, Jas and Becky all accepted.

Not having had time to explain her plan in person, Jas sent a group text round to the others that evening. **Need 2 visit Mr F again asap. Mia, can yr dad take us?**

**He says OK**, Mia texted back.

When they arrived back at the hospital – bringing grapes this time, provided by Mia's mum, instead of chocolates – they found that Mr Fortune was almost well enough to go home. 'Although I'll be hobbling for a while!' he told them.

The girls should have been pleased to hear that Mr Fortune was going home soon, but as Becky had pointed out on the way there, at least in hospital there were always people around to take care of him. Outside, he would be in a lot more danger. That, however, was where Jas's plan came in.

'Could you hire us?' she asked the record company boss. 'Like work experience or something? It'd all look dead normal, and we'd be happy to make tea or do photocopying or stuff, but really we'd be investigating!'

Mr Fortune seemed surprised, but after a moment's thought he agreed. The girls were thrilled – not only might they find some clues, but they'd be getting to see how the music business worked as well!

'As long as your parents give permission, of course,' Mr Fortune added.

None of the girls thought that would be a problem. 'Mum's always saying I should be "doing something useful" instead of hanging around the Mayfair Park all the time,' Jas said. 'She'll think it's great if I've got some work experience.'

As it turned out, all their parents were delighted – especially because, as the Fortune Records offices were within walking distance for all the girls, none of them would be called on to give lifts!

'Josh is gonna be pretty annoyed when we turn up, though,' said Lauren.

'So we're going to have to make it look really

convincing that we're just there for work experience,' Becky told her. 'I mean, come on, *we* know we're brilliant detectives, but he'll just think we're a bunch of schoolgirls. I don't think he recognized us from the news or anything, not like his dad did. It'll be fine.'

In the end it was agreed that Lauren, Becky, Mia and Jas would report to Mr Fortune in his office on Monday – the day he was planning to return to work – and stay for one week.

'A week should be plenty,' Jas said. 'We'll just have to make sure we've found some evidence by then.'

Jas felt both nervous and excited when they all arrived at Fortune Records on Monday morning. The offices were on the third floor of a tall building that contained lots of different companies. A board in the foyer listed them all. Becky excitedly pointed out her favourite fashion magazine on the fifth floor, while Mia was more interested in the computer firm on floor seven. The receptionist – a young man called Leo – was expecting them, and gave them a big smile as he phoned for someone to come and take them up to the third floor.

After a couple of minutes, Olivia Fortune

appeared out of the lift to escort them up. 'Dad wanted to come down himself,' she said, 'but he needs to use a walking stick since his accident and it takes him ages to get anywhere, so I offered to fetch you instead.' She was friendly and welcoming, and Jas wondered if Mr Fortune had told her why they were there. Probably not, she decided, so it would be better for them not to mention it either.

It soon became clear that having four girls following Mr Fortune around all day was not going to work. They got in each other's way and there weren't enough easy jobs for them all to do, although Jas was feeling pretty pleased with herself as she'd spotted Tom's demo CD at the bottom of a stack of discs on Mr Fortune's desk and moved it to the top of the pile!

After about half an hour, Jas suggested that Mia and Becky should stay with Mr Fortune, while she and Lauren went round and asked if they could help out anyone else. ('But really, we'll be looking for clues,' she whispered to Lauren.)

The record company boss agreed, and the two girls left the room. There were several other offices along the corridor they were in. On the opposite side to Mr Fortune's office was a closed door marked OLIVIA FORTUNE, and next to that was a door with JOSHUA FORTUNE written on it. That one was open.

'Look!' said Jas. 'Josh's office is empty. This is our chance!'

Lauren nodded in agreement. They hurried inside, pulling the door to so no one would see them searching, but not shutting it in case that looked suspicious. Jas started skimming through the papers on the desk, while Lauren looked along Josh's book shelves. 'Oh!' Lauren gasped suddenly. Jas hurried over. In the middle of a load of books on music there was a car repair manual – the manual for an E-Type Jaguar!

'That's the car that Mr Fortune crashed!' Jas said. 'This book'd tell Josh how the brakes work, wouldn't it? Which means he'd know how to make sure the car crashed! I reckon that proves he's the one who's doing all this.'

The two girls stared at each other. 'What do we do now?' Lauren asked.

But before Jas could answer, a voice came from the corridor outside.

'At least Dad's back at work now,' they heard Olivia say. 'If he'd had to spend much more time in hospital the Board of Directors would have had to – well, remove him from “active duty”, shall we say?’

‘He wouldn’t have liked that,’ Josh’s voice replied.

Lauren and Jas froze. Josh was just outside the door! They couldn’t leave without him seeing them – they just had to hope he was on his way somewhere else and didn’t need to come inside his office.

‘Well, I wouldn’t have liked all the extra work and responsibility,’ Olivia continued. ‘I’ve got quite enough to do right now. So it all worked out for the best.’

‘I’m not so sure,’ answered Josh. ‘I don’t think Dad needs that work or responsibility either. He refuses to consider retiring, but this is all getting too much for him. It’d be much better if he gave it up.’

Jas snorted. ‘Oh yeah, like he really cares about his dad’s health,’ she whispered.

She and Lauren had come round to the front of Josh’s desk, ready to make a move as soon as they heard the brother and sister move away. But to their horror, Olivia’s voice said, ‘See you,’ and the door to the office was pushed open!

Josh looked furious to see the girls. ‘What are you doing in here?’ he snapped.

'Mr Fortune sent us to see if we could do anything to help you,' Jas said, thinking quickly. Anyway, it was sort of the truth!

'Well, there isn't,' Josh said. 'I don't know what the old man was thinking, letting you lot in here making nuisances of yourselves.' He held the door wide open and made it clear he expected them to go through it.

'He didn't even say thank you!' Jas whispered indignantly as the door shut behind them.

They stood there for a few moments, wondering what to do next. A loud blast of music came from the other side of the door as Josh's mobile rang, and they listened as he made an appointment for lunch with whoever he was speaking to.

'I don't think we should let him out of our sight,' Jas said. 'If Mia and Becky are watching Mr Fortune and we're watching Josh, then at least nothing bad should happen.'

They found a little kitchenette nearly opposite Josh's office. By the side of the sink was a pile of dirty coffee cups. 'Brilliant, we can wash those up!' said Lauren. Jas was surprised – Lauren wasn't usually enthusiastic about cleaning! But Lauren quickly explained. 'We can keep an eye on Josh's door from here, but if anyone sees us it'll just look like we're being useful.'

'Brilliant,' Jas agreed.

Operation Josh was go!

# CHAPTER FOURTEEN

Mia and Becky were having a great time with Mr Fortune. They'd almost forgotten that they were there to carry out detective work, the music business was so fascinating! And when Mr Fortune announced that he was off to see a 4ever rehearsal and of course they must come with him, they jumped up and down with excitement! 'Go and see if your friends want to join us,' he said.

Well, *of course* Lauren and Jas would want to go too – there was no question about that! Mia and Becky found the others elbow-deep in washing-up and told them what was going on. But to their surprise, Jas gave an enormous groan.

'Oh no! We can't come – we have to keep watching Josh!' she said.

'But if we're watching Mr Fortune . . .' said Mia.

Lauren shook her head. 'We're here to be

detectives – we've got to do the job properly. Josh is our only real suspect, we have to stay close to him.' But she looked completely miserable too.

Mia and Becky couldn't tell Mr Fortune exactly why Lauren and Jas were staying behind, as they had to keep it secret that they suspected his own son was trying to hurt him. They just said the others were too busy. However, they decided they mustn't enjoy themselves at the rehearsal *too* much – it wouldn't be fair. But it soon got so exciting that they forgot all about not having a great time!

First Mr Fortune took them in a taxi to a nearby theatre, where the 4ever boys were practising for their first concert. Mia and Becky were allowed to stand in the wings of the stage to watch, and to the girls' amazement, Pete, Robin, Niall and Jason not only smiled and gave them a wave, but came over to say hello during a break. 'We met at the video shoot,' Pete said – as if they'd have forgotten! 'Becky and Mia, isn't it?'

After being remembered by 4ever, they didn't think the day could get any better – but it did! As part of their routine, Robin and Jason had to run to the front of the stage, dodging the other two on the way. However much they and their choreographer tried, though, it just looked awkward – and more than once the whole group ended up in a laughing heap on the floor.

'They should leapfrog over Niall and Pete instead,' Mia whispered to Becky, doing a mime of her idea.

Suddenly she saw that the choreographer – a stern-looking woman called Annette – was staring at her. 'What did you just say?' Annette asked.

'Nothing,' Mia mumbled, feeling like she was being told off in class for talking.

'No, really,' said Mr Fortune with a smile, '*I'd* like to hear what you were saying.'

So, utterly embarrassed, Mia told them her idea.

'Hmm,' said Annette. 'I think we'll try it.'

To Mia's astonishment, 4ever started their routine again, with Robin and Jason leapfrogging over Niall and Pete. And it worked perfectly!

'Good one!' called Jason, and Robin gave them a thumbs-up.

Now Mia was glowing with pride rather than embarrassment!

All too soon, the girls noticed Mr Fortune checking his watch. 'Sorry, Becky, Mia,' he said,

'I've got a meeting with an agent back at the office soon, so we need to leave. I thought we'd walk as I need to exercise my leg, but it takes me three times as long to get anywhere these days. Olivia keeps phoning to make sure I'm going to be back in time.'

'Lauren and Jas are going to be *so* jealous!' said Becky as the band waved goodbye to her, Mia and Mr Fortune, and Mia had to agree. Jas – who was of course 4ever's biggest fan – might never forgive them!

The three of them went out through the stage door. It led on to a little back alley – 'So the actors or singers can get out without having to push through all the crowds at the front of the theatre,' Mr Fortune explained.

With the girls on either side of him, he began to hobble across the narrow street. Suddenly he gave an exclamation of annoyance. 'Bother! I think I've left my phone in the theatre!'

'Oh, we'll get it,' Becky said. She ran off towards the stage door. Mia started to follow her, but then turned back to Mr Fortune. He was obviously finding walking difficult and she thought it might be better not to leave him.

Suddenly there was a screech as a car leaped out of nowhere. Mr Fortune, in the middle of the road, dropped his walking stick in shock.

Mia didn't stop to think. She wasn't even really aware of what she was doing. All that was in her head was that she had to save Mr Fortune. She ran forward as fast as she could, pushing him onto the far pavement.

The car roared past. Mr Fortune lay on the ground, looking frightened but not seriously hurt.

'You saved my life!' he gasped.

Mia shook her head, still a bit shocked. 'I just saw the car coming . . .' she said. 'It was going so fast . . .' She was staring in the direction the car had taken, although it was now out of sight. Could she be mistaken? Had she really seen what she thought she'd seen?

Becky came running back, the phone in her hand. 'What's happened?' she cried. 'Are you all right?'

Mr Fortune explained, with much praise of Mia's bravery and fast thinking, as the girls helped him to his feet and picked up his walking stick. But Mia's thoughts were elsewhere. No, she hadn't been mistaken, she was sure! This was the breakthrough they'd been waiting for!

Jas and Lauren's morning wasn't anywhere near as exciting as Becky and Mia's. They washed all the dirty coffee cups very slowly. Then they washed them again. Then they tidied the kitchen cupboards. Then they rearranged the spoons. Then they washed the now-very-clean cups again.

Finally, Josh emerged from his office and went to the lift. After making sure he'd pressed the DOWN button, the two girls hurried down the stairs and got to reception just in time to see Josh leave the building. They waited until he was walking down the street, then hurried after him.

Following someone in real life wasn't nearly as easy as it seemed in detective stories. Somehow, you had to stay far enough away from the person you were trailing for them not to spot you, but close enough so you didn't lose them. The only good thing, Lauren said to Jas, was that at least Josh was on foot, not driving. Then following him really would have been impossible.

Lauren found she still had her baseball cap and sunglasses in her bag, so she put those on as a disguise. At least her distinctive auburn hair was now covered up. Jas wasn't entirely sure this would work, though. 'He's already thrown one white girl and one black girl out of his office this morning,' she said. 'So if he turns round and sees one white girl and one black girl right behind him, even if one of them's now wearing a baseball cap, he's gonna smell a rat, yeah?'

'Yes, but even if he does, he'll never suspect what we're really after,' said Lauren. 'He'll just think we're a nuisance; he'll never dream we're trying to find proof that he's a criminal!'

Jas suddenly stopped still. 'Well, it doesn't matter anyway. Look where he's gone.' Josh had suddenly disappeared through the door of an extremely posh restaurant. 'We can't follow him in there, can we?' said Jas.

Lauren grinned. 'Oh, I don't see why not . . .'

Followed by a nervous Jas, she marched up to the restaurant and walked in. A bow-tied maître d' immediately stepped in front of them. 'I don't think this is the sort of place you kids want to be hanging around in,' he said with a sneer.

But Lauren had seen a lot of famous people at the Mayfair Park, and she knew how to act. She took off her dark glasses and stared at him as if he were a particularly disgusting slug. 'Oh, really?' she said. 'Maybe you'd like me to take my business elsewhere? You do know who I am, don't you?'

He looked a bit taken aback, but didn't move

to let them in. Luckily, Jas had obviously worked out what Lauren was getting at. 'You mean you haven't seen *Where Two Rivers Meet*, or *The Angel Princess*?' she said, naming two recent hit films. She turned to Lauren. 'Guess we'd better go somewhere else, then.' She got out her phone. 'I'll call your director, let him know that we'll be meeting him at a different restaurant. Is there anywhere round here where the staff have manners?'

'I've heard the Mayfair Park Hotel's pretty good,' Lauren said, trying not to laugh.

The waiter forced a smile onto his face. 'I'm sorry, miss,' he said to Lauren. 'Didn't recognize you with the glasses on – please come right in.' Lauren and Jas stifled giggles as they followed him inside.

Josh was at a table with two other men, both in suits, with briefcases by their feet. Unfortunately, he was sitting facing into the restaurant, so he would be able to see them wherever they sat. Or at least he would if they sat in the main area . . .

'Er, we'll just wait at the bar, I think,' Lauren said. 'Until the rest of our party arrives.' The man reluctantly ushered them to a pair of stools in the bar area.

'That was brilliant, Lols!' Jas said as they shuffled along until they had a good view of Josh's back.

'How dare you talk to me!' said Lauren, still in her 'famous' voice. 'Don't you know who I am?' Then she burst out laughing.

Jas laughed too as she reached out and picked up a drinks menu. Suddenly the laughter stopped. 'Oh wow!' she said. 'Look at the prices! I don't think we can even afford a Coke!'

They both emptied their purses, and then scrabbled through their pockets and bags just in case there were any loose coins floating around. Jas sorted the coins into piles and counted it all up. 'OK, I was wrong,' she said at last. 'We *can* afford a Coke. Just one between us, though. Let's hope Josh's meeting's going to be a quick one . . .'

As the barman came over to take their order, they spotted a waiter carrying three huge plates of steak and chips to Josh and his companions. 'Oh dear,' said Lauren. 'It looks like he's going to be here a while.' She looked up at the barman and gave her best 'celebrity' pout. 'One Coke,' she said. 'And two straws . . .'

They were sipping at their drink as slowly as possible – could they really make one Coke last several hours? – when Jas's phone rang. She answered it, and Lauren watched an expression of amazement cross her face.

'That was Mia,' said Jas, when she finally clicked off the mobile. 'She says someone's just tried to run over Mr Fortune – and she knows who it was!'

'It was a silver Mercedes that tried to run over Mr Fortune,' said Mia, 'and its registration number ended in JAS. It was the car we saw at Mr Fortune's house, the one that belongs to Josh.'

Mia, Becky, Lauren and Jas were gathered outside the Fortune Records office building. Lauren and Jas had arrived just in time to see Terry driving Mr Fortune away. 'Poor Mr Fortune's gone back to hospital,' Becky explained. 'His leg was hurt again when he fell. And he went a bit wobbly.'

'I don't blame him,' said Mia.

Jas looked at Mia and realized with concern that her friend was beginning to shiver.

'I'm sorry!' Mia said, her voice shaking a bit. 'I don't know why I'm being so silly, it's all over now . . .'

Becky began to explain to the others exactly what had happened.

Lauren threw her arms round Mia. 'You were so brave!' she said. 'I could never have done that!'

'You might've been killed!' Jas gasped in horror. She led Mia over to a bench, and the other girl smiled her thanks as she sat down. Jas and Lauren sat on either side of their friend, their arms around her shoulders.

Becky didn't sit down. She stood in front of them, her face hard. 'This is getting really serious,' she said. 'You're right, Jas. Mia might've been killed, and so might Mr Fortune. We can't let anything else happen. We *have* to get to the bottom of this mystery.'

'But what do we do?' asked Lauren. 'We know it's not Josh after all. We've been watching him the whole time. He couldn't possibly have just tried to run over his dad.'

'Maybe someone else has got a car just like it,' suggested Jas.

Mia shook her head. 'Not with the same numberplate.'

'I know,' said Becky. 'Josh would've parked in the underground car park. Let's go and see if his car's there – if you're OK, Mia?'

Mia nodded. 'I'm fine,' she said.

So they went back to the office building and

took the lift down to the basement level. One row of spaces was labelled FORTUNE RECORDS, and the silver Mercedes wasn't difficult to spot.

'There, it can't have been Josh's car you saw, Mia,' Lauren said again.

Mia went over to the Mercedes and touched the bonnet. 'It's still warm,' she said. She turned to the others, her eyes glowing. 'It *was* Josh's car I saw – but it can't have been Josh who was driving it! It's someone else who's trying to harm Mr Fortune!'

It was a few moments before anyone else spoke. Becky finally broke the silence. 'It doesn't look like anyone's broken into the car,' she said.

Jas slapped her forehead. 'Duh!' she said. 'I've just remembered – I saw a key on Josh's desk this morning – and the fob had the Mercedes logo on it! It would have been easy for someone to just take the key off his desk . . .'

'So it must be someone who's been in the office this morning!' Mia realized.

Lauren's mind was whirring. 'I think I've finally worked it out,' she said. 'It's not Josh who's trying to get rid of his father – it's Olivia!'

'What?' Mia, Jas and Becky sounded amazed.

'But Olivia always seemed so worried about

her dad,' said Mia. 'Josh never seemed to care. And all the clues pointed to him . . .'

Lauren was nodding eagerly. 'Yes! That's the point! I think Josh was framed!'

'What, like a picture?' asked Jas.

'I mean,' said Lauren, 'that it was deliberate. Someone else was arranging it so Josh seemed to be guilty. And the person who'd have the most opportunity to do that would be his sister – they even work together!'

Mia was looking thoughtful. 'Do you remember when Mr Fortune was eating the Mississippi Mud Pie at the party? He said to Olivia that it was very kind of her to think of getting it for him!'

'Really?' said Becky. 'It was Josh who asked me to get a dessert, but I guess Olivia might have suggested the idea to him – *and* she took the pie from me when I brought it back.'

'But how could she have poisoned the pie in a room full of people without anyone noticing?' asked Jas.

No one had an answer to that question.

'She could easily have sent her dad the poisoned chocolates, though,' said Becky. 'Just as easily as Josh or Mr Star. And we know she has a key to the garage where the Jaguar was kept.

She could have borrowed that car manual Lauren and Jas saw in Josh's office, and cut the brakes. But the big question is – why?'

Lauren's brow creased with concentration. 'There was that bit in the paper,' she said. 'You know, about Josh and Olivia taking over Fortune Records when their dad retires. But Mr Fortune says he's not going to retire. Maybe Olivia's fed up with waiting.'

'That's it,' said Mia. 'With Mr Fortune in hospital, or – or, well, you know, something worse – Olivia and Josh would be put in charge of the business.'

'And Becky's right,' said Jas eagerly. 'Olivia's set it all up so it looks like Josh did it. So if anyone got suspicious and realized all those things weren't accidents, it'd be Josh who'd get arrested, not her.'

'And then,' added Lauren, 'she'd be in charge. Just her. She'd be the boss of Fortune Records – the only boss.'

The four of them stood in silence. It was a horrible thought. Olivia seemed so nice, but they were now convinced that she was the one who had been plotting to hurt her father all along.

* * *

'Right,' said Jas. 'Let's see if Olivia's in her office. We've gotta be sure it's her. We ought to check if she's got an alibi.'

They took the lift up to the Fortune Records floor, and knocked on Olivia's door. 'Come in,' her voice called from the other side.

Mr Fortune's daughter was looking a bit flustered as they walked in. 'Are you OK?' Jas asked.

'Oh, yes, yes – just worried about the old man,' she said. She gave them a sweet smile. 'It seems to be one thing after another – he's so accident-prone. I've just called Josh to let him know. He'll be back in a minute. Goodness knows where my brother's been – I did try to get hold of him, but he was obviously too busy to answer.'

Jas found it hard to smile back at her. She was sure Olivia was lying – Jas had heard Josh's mobile go off and knew it had a very loud ring tone; she was certain she'd have known if it had rung while they were following him earlier. Olivia was just trying to make it look like Josh might have been out driving his car, while she was back in her office trying to phone him! Not a very convincing alibi!

'Were you very busy this morning too?' said

Mia. 'We never realized how much work people had to do in the music business.'

Olivia looked a little bit startled at the question, but answered almost straight away. 'Oh yes, I've been preparing a Powerpoint presentation all day.' She pointed at her computer, which was showing a Powerpoint screen. 'Do you want to see it?'

'Thanks,' said Jas, 'but we'd better not bother you any longer. We just wanted to see if you were all right – with your dad being hurt again and everything.'

They'd found out exactly what they wanted to know. Olivia was far too keen to show them her Powerpoint presentation – that was very suspicious. As far as they were concerned, their new main suspect didn't have a proper alibi at all!

The girls left Olivia's office.

'She did it!' Jas declared as they walked back towards the lift. 'Did you see how worried she looked? Especially when Mia asked her if she'd been busy this morning.'

Mia frowned. 'If I could get a look at her computer, I could probably tell if she was working at it when someone was driving at Mr

Fortune,' she said. 'But I don't think I'm going to get a chance.'

'Bet she wasn't, though,' said Lauren.

At that moment, the lift *ping*ed, and Josh came out, a tall woman beside him. 'Thank you for agreeing to meet with me instead of my father,' he was saying to her. 'Unfortunately, on his way back to the office to see you, he was in an accident and has had to go to hospital.'

Olivia's door opened and she came out into the corridor. 'Oh, Ms Johnson,' she said. 'Leo just called up to say you were here. I wondered if you'd be happy to meet with me as Dad's not available.'

'It's all right, Liv,' Josh said. 'Dad called from the ambulance and asked me to come back from lunch and take the meeting.'

Olivia nodded and went back inside her office.

'Did you see her face?' Lauren whispered to the others. 'She looked really furious.'

At that moment Josh spotted the four girls standing about in the corridor – but instead of snapping at them as he usually did, he gave a weak smile. 'Would one of you girls mind fetching us some coffee?' he said.

'I'll do it,' said Jas.

He nodded his thanks. 'Then you might as well all go off home. I'm afraid we're going to be a bit too busy with my father in hospital to find jobs for you to do.'

Becky, Lauren and Mia headed to the lift, telling Jas they'd meet her in the foyer. Jas went into the little kitchenette and put the kettle on to boil. Luckily, after that morning, she knew where everything was! There was a cafetière on the side, and she got ground coffee beans out of the fridge, along with a carton of milk. She put two cups on a tray with a bowl of sugar, poured milk into a milk jug and boiling water into the cafetière, thinking that it was almost as posh as the coffee at the Mayfair Park Hotel! Then she carried the tray to Josh's office.

Josh thanked her briefly as she put the tray down on his desk. He was talking to the tall woman, who was obviously a friend as well as a client, and Jas's ears pricked up when she heard what he was saying. She had been going to leave the tray and go, but now she pushed the plunger down on the cafetière and began to serve the coffee so she could stay a few moments longer.

'Yes, it's doing my head in,' he was saying. 'In fact I've been so worried I can hardly think about anything else. I've found myself so bad-tempered, snapping at everyone, but I just can't sleep for worrying about Dad. I wanted to get him a wonderful birthday present to cheer him up after that food-poisoning incident, and when Olivia suggested a classic car, that seemed perfect.' His face lit up. 'We both love cars, Dad and me. Olivia even gave me a manual for the Jaguar I chose – she said Dad and I could do up the car together.' Now he was pointing at the book Jas and Lauren had spotted earlier, and his expression was serious. 'But before I'd even had a chance to look at the book, he had his accident. If only I'd been able to check the car over first!'

Having poured the coffee, Jas made a hasty exit. She was so excited by what she'd heard – it was Olivia who'd suggested getting Mr Fortune the car which had crashed, and she'd even given her brother the manual, 'framing' him, as Lauren would have put it. The others would want to know all this!

Mia, Lauren and Becky were waiting for Jas in the foyer, as they'd arranged. Jas joined them and they decided to leave the building and go to the park, where they could speak privately.

'So, Josh seemed really upset about his dad,'

Jas said as she finished her story. 'He's only been rude to us because he's been so worried. Olivia's the one behind it all!'

'We can't tell Mr Fortune; we can't tell anyone!' Mia said. 'It all makes sense, but we still don't have any proof. And anyway, he wouldn't believe us. I mean, *my* dad'd never believe *I'd* try to poison him or anything.'

'Yeah, although you did make him eat that banana custard you made in Food Tech,' Jas pointed out with a grin.

'At least we know Olivia's nowhere near her dad at the moment,' said Lauren as Mia pouted at her friend. 'But we can't watch them all the time. We've got to go home in the evenings at least!'

'I'm just thinking,' said Becky. 'Hold on a moment.' Mia, Lauren and Jas waited patiently. Finally Becky spoke. 'It's all been arranged really carefully,' she said. 'Olivia might be framing Josh, but that's only a sort of safeguard – I don't think she really wants *anyone* to be suspected. The chocolates were the first thing, before anyone dreamed anything suspicious might be going on, and she was probably the one who got rid of the evidence afterwards. Then there was the Mississippi Mud Pie at the party. Well, everyone thought that was food poisoning, even after the environmental health officer's report. The car crash appeared to be an accident, like there'd just been something wrong with a very old car. And today it would have seemed like a hit and run, the sort that are in the papers all the time, if Mia hadn't recognized the car.'

'So – what're you saying?' asked Jas.

'I'm saying that Olivia won't act again until she has another chance to make it look like an accident,' Becky told her. 'She won't try to run him down again – it'd look too suspicious. She won't send chocolates – Mr Fortune would never eat anything he gets in the post, not a second time. And she won't visit him at home and try anything, because she'd be the obvious suspect. She'll wait for an opportunity to engineer another "accident". That's what we've got to watch out for.'

The others nodded. It made sense. But keeping Mr Fortune safe still wasn't going to be easy.

They all went home. Lauren went up to the Bonds' flat at the Mayfair Park, her mind whirling. What were they going to do?

'You look a bit tired,' her dad said. 'Is the music business hard work?'

'I hope you're not fed up with it already,' put in her mum. 'We've got the 4ever launch party here on Saturday.'

Lauren stared. 'We've got *what*?'

'Oh, I thought you'd know, working there,' said Mrs Bond with a smile. 'While we were arranging the party for after the video shoot, Samuel Fortune spoke about holding a party for the release of the group's first single. Well, as soon as we had the clean bill of health from the inspectors, I got in touch and offered to host the party for nothing. A sort of apology – even though his illness wasn't our fault at all – plus good publicity and a way to show the world that the Mayfair Park Hotel is perfectly safe in every way.'

'That daughter of his – Olivia, is it? – rang up and accepted on his behalf this afternoon,' said Mr Bond.

*Oh no.* It was suddenly all horribly clear to Lauren. This was Olivia's new plan. It was just like Becky had said: she was waiting for a chance to create another 'accident'. There had already been one 'food poisoning' incident at the Mayfair Park, now there would be another.

But if she succeeded, it wouldn't just be Mr Fortune who got hurt. The Mayfair Park Hotel would be ruined for ever!

# CHAPTER SIXTEEN

Lauren spent most of the evening trying to persuade her mum to call off the party, but Mrs Bond wouldn't listen to her. When Lauren suggested that there might be another poisoning incident, Mrs Bond got very cross indeed. 'My kitchens are perfectly clean!' she insisted angrily, and it all ended in a row, which wasn't what Lauren had planned at all.

**We have to tell police**, she texted Becky, but wasn't surprised to receive the reply, **We need proof first!**

She met up with the others in the park the next day, not wanting to hang around the Mayfair Park, while her mum was still unhappy with her. Luckily Mia brought Tumble along, and the dog's obvious joy at seeing them all soon cheered Lauren up.

She was surprised to see that the others weren't as worried by the news of the party as she had been. It was Jas who summed it up. 'We know what Olivia's planning,' she said, 'but she doesn't know we know. And she's making a big mistake if she tries something else at the Mayfair Park, 'cos that's our territory. Ms Olivia Fortune doesn't know what she's up against!'

'We'll never let her out of our sight,' Becky said. 'We'll get Charlie to help too, and Joe.'

'And Tom,' Mia suggested. 'The more people the better.'

'Good one,' Becky said. 'Right, this is what we do . . .'

Lauren concentrated hard as Becky outlined their strategy. Becky treated every plan like a military operation, and expected the other girls to pay attention!

Becky and Jas would be Tailing Team One. They would follow Olivia at the party. But as Olivia knew what they looked like and might become suspicious, Charlie and Joe – whom she'd never met – would be Tailing Team Two, also watching Olivia's every move. Mia, Lauren and Tom would be the perimeter team, ready to leap into action if Olivia left the main party, paying special attention to any trip that might take her near the kitchens.

'The trouble is,' said Becky, 'we still have no

idea how she managed to poison the pie, so we don't know what to watch for.'

At that moment Tumble ran up, barking excitedly for Mia to follow him. She went off to see what the matter was, and came back a minute later, laughing. 'Lauren, look what Tumble's found!' she said. 'It's your missing watch – it must have fallen off here.' She held it up by the strap. 'Tumble must have come across it and recognized your smell! Isn't he clever?'

They all made a fuss of Tumble, who licked their faces happily.

Mia suddenly had an idea. 'I know!' she said excitedly. 'Dogs are brilliant at sniffing out stuff – the police use them and everything. I bet Tumble could detect if Olivia had poison with her at the party! If we found the poison before she managed to use it, it would be a lot safer for everyone.'

The others agreed it was worth a try.

The hospital had told Mr Fortune to rest at home after his fall, which meant an end to the girls' 'work experience' at Fortune Records. But as they were pretty sure he would be safe until the party, they didn't mind too much. 'Although it would have been nice to meet some more bands,' said Jas.

Charlie and Joe were thrilled to have a chance to be proper spies, and spent the week practising. Kyle, the bar manager, complained to Mrs Bond that they had taken all his lemons to make invisible ink – just in case they had to send secret messages, although Lauren told them it wasn't really likely – and the hotel guests got used to seeing two boys wandering through the lobby in various disguises.

Tom was also happy to help out, so everything was on track. Becky went over their instructions again and again, and by Saturday night they were all completely clear on what they had to do.

When the party started, Tailing Team One – Becky and Jas – waited by the ballroom doors, saying hello to guests as they arrived. Mr Fortune, still walking with a stick, greeted them cheerfully. Josh, following him, only grunted at their welcome, but the girls didn't mind so much now they knew it was worry that was making him so grumpy.

'Here she comes!' Jas whispered as Olivia approached the doors. Becky was pleased to see she was wearing a sunflower-yellow cocktail dress – it would make her very easy to spot among the crowds. But when Olivia gave them a charming smile and said how pleased she was to be back at the Mayfair Park Hotel, Becky had a sudden wobble. Had they got it all wrong? Could Olivia really be the person who had been doing such dreadful things? But she took a deep breath, remembering all the evidence they'd uncovered. Yes. She was sure they were right.

Jas and Becky kept close to Olivia as she went round the room, exchanging words with lots of different people. Today there were no trays of canapés; instead Mrs Bond had arranged two large tables covered with food. Becky spotted a pair of binoculars poking round the edge of the white tablecloth hanging down from one of the buffet tables, and she smiled. Tailing Team Two – Charlie and Joe – were in position!

Rather sooner than they'd hoped, Olivia seemed to become aware that Tailing Team One was always nearby. Her sunny smile began to fade, and she darted annoyed looks at them. Time for Tailing Team Two to come out of cover and take over. Becky gave the agreed signal – three tugs on her left earlobe – and a moment later she saw Charlie and Joe pop up from behind the buffet table. Both were in their best 'James Bond' evening dress – black suit, white shirt and bow tie – and, to Becky's amusement, both were sipping blackcurrant squash from cocktail glasses. 'Shaken – not stirred,' Charlie murmured as the boys went past.

Meanwhile, Tom was going round the party with a tray of drinks. Lauren, on guard at the edge of the room, saw Olivia take a glass of wine, and watched closely in case she tried to put anything in it and pass it to her father. But Olivia just drank it herself and put the empty glass on the buffet table. She then picked up a plate and began to help herself to smoked salmon and salad. Lauren had a moment of panic. Was this it? Was Olivia going to poison some of the food on her plate and offer it to Mr Fortune?

Mia and Tumble were waiting in the small office at the bottom of the stairs, where Lauren had earlier put a beanbag, and bowls of water and dog biscuits. So far they'd had no chance to try out Tumble as a sniffer dog, but although it was a very long shot, anything had to be worth trying.

Lauren sent a quick text to Mia, then took a

deep breath and went over to Olivia. 'Excuse me, Ms Fortune,' she said politely. 'There's a phone call for you. Would you mind coming with me for a moment?'

Olivia smiled politely, popped an olive in her mouth and, still carrying her plate, followed Lauren out of the ballroom and along the corridor to the small office.

Tumble gave a bark of happiness when Lauren opened the door, which made Olivia jump and shy away. Gwen was obviously right – she wasn't very keen on dogs. But to Lauren's disappointment, Tumble showed no interest in Olivia at all. Well, it wasn't like he was a trained sniffer dog – he probably couldn't detect poison after all. But then suddenly . . .

As Mia led Tumble nearer, he started to bark excitedly. Mia kept a hold on his collar as he began to jump about, trying to get close to the young woman. Olivia backed away. 'Keep that horrid mutt away from me!' she shrieked. Lauren and Mia looked at each other in astonishment – it was working! Tumble was going to find the poison for them! At a nod from Lauren, Mia let go of the dog and they held their breath . . .

. . . then let it out again in disappointment as Tumble pounced eagerly on the smoked salmon that had dropped from Olivia's plate when she jumped.

'I thought there was supposed to be a phone call for me?' Olivia demanded. 'I take it you didn't bring me here just so this revolting animal could harass me.'

Lauren had to stop herself laughing, as of course that was exactly why they had brought her there!

'I'm really sorry,' Mia said, indicating the telephone on the desk, 'the person's rung off and they didn't give their name.'

Olivia sniffed in disgust and turned on her heel. 'It's appalling, allowing animals in a hotel like this. It's so unhygienic, it's a wonder we don't all come down with food poisoning! I shall complain to the manager!' she called over her shoulder as she stormed back to the ballroom.

'Not so friendly now, is she?' said Lauren.

'I'm sorry,' said Mia. 'Tumble always goes for any food that falls on the floor. Do you think Olivia really will complain to your dad?'

'I'm sure she will,' said Lauren. 'It'll make her story of food poisoning seem more convincing. But don't worry. We won't get into trouble, not after we've revealed her as the true poisoner.'

Mia nodded, but she still looked worried.

'I reckon Olivia'll be staying in the ballroom for now,' Lauren carried on. 'Will Tumble be OK here on his own if you come back in with me?'

Mia nodded again. 'Yeah, he'll be all right for a while – he's got the beanbag and food and everything, and it's not like it's for ever . . .'

Lauren suddenly gasped. '*For ever!* I've been so busy worrying about Olivia that I forgot – 4ever will be performing their new single any minute now! We've got to get back!'

Luckily, they hadn't missed anything, although at one end of the ballroom a space had been cleared, with spotlights and microphones arranged ready for 4ever's performance.

Lauren and Mia met up with Becky and Jas.

'Nothing to report,' Becky said. 'What about you? Olivia looked really annoyed when she got back.'

'Yeah, but Tumble didn't find any poison on her,' said Lauren. 'Maybe we've got it wrong. Maybe she's not going to try tonight after all.' But really, she was convinced that something was going to happen.

Jas nudged Lauren. Olivia had joined Mr Fortune and Josh. She said a word to Josh, who went over to the buffet table and began to fill a plate with food.

'It's all sweet stuff,' said Jas. 'D'you reckon Olivia's told him to get food for Mr Fortune – like last time – so he's the one who comes under suspicion, not her?'

It looked like that was the case, as Josh came back and offered the plate to his father. Mr Fortune, unable to balance a plate, a fork and his walking stick, sat down on a chair. Josh put the plate on a side table beside him.

'Olivia's standing next to them – but she's not touched the food,' Becky said. 'Not yet, anyway. We've got to keep watching. Jas and I'll stay over here and watch Olivia. Lauren, Mia, go and stand behind Mr Fortune and don't take your eyes off his plate. Quick, you'd better get in position before the band comes on.'

Lauren and Mia began to circle round the ballroom so that the Fortunes wouldn't see them approaching. But just as they were nearing Mr Fortune, the lights went out! 'Oh no!' gasped Lauren. They were too late – the band was about to sing! A voice boomed: 'Ladies and gentlemen, please welcome Pete, Jason, Niall and Robin – 4ever!'

The girls peered through the gloom. 'Olivia

must have been waiting for this!' whispered Lauren to Mia. 'She thinks no one will be watching her! Come on, we've got to get closer.'

There was a roar from the audience as 4ever came forward, but none of the girls cheered – they were too busy concentrating on the job in hand. Dazzled by the sudden spotlights, Mia and Lauren now couldn't see a thing in the ballroom. They were still trying to get closer to the Fortunes but kept bumping into chairs or tripping over feet as they stumbled through the audience.

Finally their vision began to clear, and they got near enough to Mr Fortune to see what was going on. To their relief, Olivia didn't appear to have moved or gone near the plate of food. Lauren held her breath as she saw Olivia reach into her handbag, but all she brought out was a little bottle of perfume. She began to spray it on to her wrists.

Mr Fortune's plate was on the table, piled high with goodies. The old man hadn't touched any of them yet, though. As the cheering died away, Lauren heard Josh say, 'Oh Dad, do you still not fancy chocolates? Well, don't want them to go to waste.' And Mr Fortune's son picked up a chocolate truffle from the plate.

'Oh, all right,' Mr Fortune replied. 'I'll try to eat something.' His hand reached out . . .

Jas had got her night vision now. She was staring as hard as she could across the dim room, and also saw Olivia spraying her perfume. It seemed perfectly innocent. She wasn't touching Mr Fortune's food.

And then Jas realized that Olivia was holding the bottle at a strange angle. The perfume wasn't falling onto her wrists – she'd sprayed most of it onto Mr Fortune's plate!

'Becky, look!' Jas cried. 'That's the poison!' The two girls ran forward, shouting, but the band had begun to sing and no one could hear them above the music.

Suddenly Jas found herself under a spotlight. She had run onto the stage area! As 4ever watched in astonishment, she grabbed Pete's microphone and yelled into it: 'Mr Fortune! Don't eat that food!'

Becky took hold of a spotlight and swung it round, lighting up a horrified Olivia, perfume bottle held high. Mr Fortune's hand was still poised over his plate.

Lauren and Mia realized what had happened

and took action. Lauren charged straight into Olivia as Mia grabbed the bottle from her hand. The woman fell backwards, knocking into the table. The plate of food fell to the floor.

But even before Jas had started yelling, Josh had popped the chocolate truffle into his mouth. Now, with the spotlight on him, and everyone in the room turning to watch, Josh fell to the floor, clutching his throat.

The girls were too late.

# CHAPTER SEVENTEEN

Someone had put on the main lights and now everyone was crowding around Josh, who was lying on the floor. Charlie and Joe, who had still been on Tailing Team duty, sped out to find a phone and call an ambulance.

'Not again – oh, not again!' Mrs Bond was muttering, looking as if she might start to cry.

Lauren ran up to her, their row forgotten. 'Don't worry, Mum. It wasn't the hotel's fault – and we can prove it.'

Suddenly Lauren heard an excited bark. Was that Tumble? She turned to look – and cried out in horror. Tumble had somehow got out of the office and was heading straight for the poisoned food strewn all over the floor.

Mia, Jas and Becky turned to see what was going on. 'Tumble! No!' Mia shouted and started to run. She wasn't going to make it in time. But someone else had seen what was happening.

Tom, the only person in the room apart from the girls who realized that the food was poisoned, leaped into action. He vaulted over a table, grabbing Tumble just as the dog was about to lick up a great big mouthful of squashed gateau.

The four girls sighed in relief.

Charlie and Joe came back in. 'An ambulance is on its way,' said Charlie, sounding very proud of himself.

'And the police too,' added Joe.

Charlie looked at Tumble. The dog was in Tom's arms, happily licking the waiter's face. 'Sorry,' he said. 'Tumble woke up when we went in the office to use the phone, and he ran out. We thought he'd probably gone to find Mia.'

At the mention of the police, Olivia had collapsed into a chair. Mr Fortune was ignoring her, caring only about his sick son. Luckily the paramedics soon arrived and said they thought Josh would be fine – he hadn't eaten enough to make him really ill. They would take him to hospital, though, just to make sure.

The police turned up just as the paramedics were leaving. Mia handed them the perfume bottle, and the police – and everyone else – listened in amazement as Lauren, Becky, Jas and Mia told the whole story.

Mr Fortune was horrified. 'I can't believe it,' he said. 'My own daughter did this to me! Why, Olivia, why?'

Between sobs, Olivia began to explain. She'd been working for Fortune Records for years, and was desperate to be in charge. But Mr Fortune was determined not to retire – he never even took a day off sick. All she'd wanted to do was to make him a bit unwell so he'd have to take some time off. Maybe that way he would realize that she was capable of running things. Maybe he'd also realize that not being at work was OK, and think about retiring after all. If he was off work for long enough, the board might even put her in charge for good . . .

But her plan went wrong. 'Nothing kept you off work. The cherry fondants made you sick, but you came straight back!' she said. 'You're like one of those toys – however much you hit them they just bounce straight back! I knew I'd have to hit harder and harder . . . I cut the brakes of the Jaguar and you could barely walk but you still wouldn't even let me take your meetings. That made me so mad . . .'

'You're telling us,' murmured Jas. 'Completely loopy, if you ask me.'

'I had to do something . . .' Olivia continued.

'I knew you'd be heading back to the office after the theatre, so I got Josh's car . . .'

She didn't finish the sentence. It seemed even Olivia couldn't find a plausible way of explaining how running over her father had seemed a good idea at the time.

Olivia began laughing hysterically. 'But even though you were hurt, even though you went to hospital, it was Josh you got to take your meeting, not me – and Josh isn't even *interested* in the music business! He hates it! It should have been me! This party was my last chance . . . But I didn't mean to really hurt you – I didn't, I didn't!' She put her head in her hands.

'If it hadn't been for these young girls, I think someone might have got very hurt indeed,' said one of the policemen. He stepped forward. 'Olivia Fortune, I think you'd better come with us to the police station . . .'

After Olivia had gone, the girls gathered around Mr Fortune. He looked so sad.

'I believe her,' he said. 'I believe that Olivia never meant to really hurt me. She's still my daughter, however disturbed she may be, and I can forgive her for what she did to me – she didn't really know what she was doing. But I find it harder to forgive her for risking so many other lives. It was pure luck that no one else got seriously hurt. Even this lovely dog was nearly poisoned.' He looked up at Tumble, still cradled in Tom's arms, and he frowned for a moment, as if trying to remember something. But then he turned to the girls again. 'I can't thank you enough,' he said. 'When you offered to help me out – well, I suppose I was just humouring you, really. I didn't dream I might be placing you in danger. But you've proved yourselves to be brave and resourceful as well as excellent detectives.'

Mrs Bond came forward. 'I've called a taxi for you, Mr Fortune,' she said. 'Let's take you up to the lobby to wait for it. I'm sure you're eager to get home.'

But Mr Fortune shook his head. 'I must go to the hospital,' he said. 'There were dark moments when I suspected my dear son Josh was responsible for my accidents – he seemed so angry all the time. I must go to him now and ask for his forgiveness.'

Mr and Mrs Bond helped the old man out of the ballroom, and the other guests began to leave.

The girls looked at each other. Another case was over – the Case of the Poisoned Pie. But solving the mystery hadn't made them feel very happy.

Then Pete, Jason, Niall and Robin came up to them – and each member of 4ever gave one of the girls a kiss on the cheek!

'We were told we'd be the stars of this party – but I reckon it's you who're the stars,' Jason told them, handing out signed copies of their new CD to the delighted girls.

'Yeah, you're definitely the heroes!' said Niall.

'You saved Mr Fortune,' Robin said with a grin.

'Three cheers for Becky, Lauren, Mia and Jas!' called Pete, and led the others as they shouted out: 'Hip hip hoorah! Hip hip hoorah! Hip hip hoorah!'

Smiling at last, and with the cheers ringing in their ears, the girls went happily up to Lauren's flat for a long talk about what had happened – and a large amount of definitely-not-poisoned chocolate cake.

# CHAPTER EIGHTEEN

It was the last week of the summer holidays, and the girls were sitting in their favourite spot in the park. Tumble was with them, of course. Mia sighed. 'I won't be able to take Tumble for walks very much when we're back at school,' she said. 'I hope he'll be all right.'

'It's so sad that no one will give him a home,' said Lauren, and the others agreed.

'Lauren, Becky, Mia, Jas! Hello!'

The girls turned to see who was calling them. Mr Fortune was walking slowly across the park, leaning on his stick. They got up to meet him, and all five sat down on a bench together. 'I've just come from the Mayfair Park Hotel,' he told them, 'and Mrs Bond told me where I might find you. I thought you might like to hear what's been happening.'

They nodded. Mia was pleased to see that Mr Fortune was smiling, and hoped what he had to tell them was good news.

It was. Josh was fine, he told them, and a lot happier now he was no longer worried about accidents happening to his dad – and also because he wasn't having to hide the fact that he hated the music business!

'How could anyone hate the music business?' said Jas. 'It's brilliant!' They all laughed.

Mr Fortune gave them a sad smile. 'I've learned that it's possible to love the music business too much,' he said. 'But Olivia's getting the professional help she needs. I've arranged for her to be transferred to a private institution where she will be very well looked after. Maybe away from the stress of the office she will begin to be more like the daughter I remember. But this has all made me realize that I was spending too much time at work. I didn't have time for other things – such as paying attention to my children. I should have realized how unhappy Olivia was, and that Josh was only working at Fortune Records to please me.' His smile became happier. 'So I've decided to retire after all!'

'But what's going to happen to your company, if you're retiring?' Jas asked.

Mr Fortune explained that it was going to merge with Star Music Group and become Star

Fortunes! Mr Star would be in charge – although Mr Fortune would still have a say in things, if he wanted to.

'What about Josh?' said Becky.

Mr Fortune beamed. 'Josh and I are going to run a classic car business! It's something we both love. It'll be more of a hobby for me, though. I'm going to spend more time at home. I was thinking of getting a dog. That's something else Josh and I share, you know, a love of dogs.' He leaned down and patted Tumble. 'I just hope I'll be able to find a dog as lovely as your one here.'

Mia gasped. She'd just had the most marvellous idea – and looking at the others, she suspected they were thinking the same thing!

'Tumble isn't my dog,' she said excitedly. 'He lives at the animal shelter. No one will give him a home because he's old and can't walk properly. But he's the friendliest, sweetest dog in the whole world . . .'

Mr Fortune held out a hand to Tumble, who sniffed it happily. 'What do you say, feller?' he said. 'I'm old and, at the moment, I can't walk properly either. But I don't think that's any reason to throw a person – or a dog – on the scrap heap. I would be honoured if you would let me give you a home.'

Tumble gave a bark of joy. 'He says yes!' cried Mia. 'Oh, thank you, Mr Fortune! Thank you so much! This is the best thing that could possibly happen!' She threw her arms round him.

Mr Fortune laughed in delight. 'I'll get in touch with the animal shelter and sort it all out,' he said as Mia finally let go. 'I have a feeling Tumble and I will be very happy together.' He got up to leave. 'Oh, by the way, before I go, I should have mentioned why I was at the Mayfair Park Hotel. As our last party was interrupted, I thought we should have another one. A big one. A very big party to celebrate the creation of Star Fortunes – and of course, to celebrate 4ever's first single going straight to number one in the charts!'

Lauren, Mia, Becky and Jas all cheered – but there was even more to come. 'There'll be lots of bands there, of course,' said Mr Fortune, 'but I was rather hoping that you would be our guests of honour. All the stars I represent want to meet you . . .'

The girls stopped cheering – they were speechless!

'Just one thing,' Mr Fortune added. 'I hope your mother won't be too upset at having to hire a new waiter for the party, Lauren.'

The girls frowned. Whatever did he mean?

'The thing is,' Mr Fortune continued, 'seeing that young waiter rescue your dog – my dog, I hope I'll soon be able to say! – reminded me that he'd given me a CD. Eating that poisoned pie put it right out of my mind. But I found it on the top of a pile in my office' – Jas grinned – 'and listened to it – and Star Fortunes has found its first ever client!'

With that, he waved and walked off.

Jas was the first to speak. 'Wow,' she said. 'We thought Mr Fortune looked like Father Christmas – and now it's like Christmas has come early! Tom's going to be famous!'

'And Tumble will have a lovely new home,' said Mia.

'And we're going to meet loads and loads of stars!' added Becky.

Lauren smiled. '*And* we're fully booked for months because 4ever told a reporter that the Mayfair Park's the best hotel in the world!'

'Well it is,' said Becky. 'We knew that already. Hurrah for the Mayfair Park Hotel!'

'Hurrah!' they all cheered. 'Hurrah for the Mayfair Park Hotel!'

'Woof,' barked Tumble. 'Woof woof woof!'

Read on for a special bonus extract from the Mayfair Park girls' first mystery:

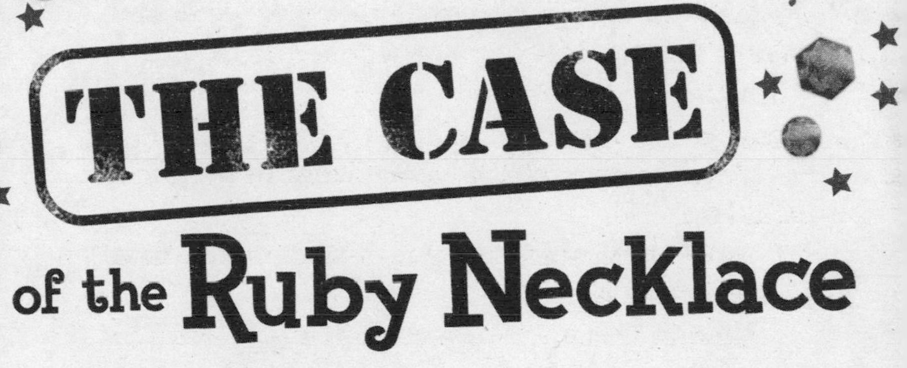

Clutching her phone in one hand, Becky loitered just inside the hotel entrance, trying to make herself look as small and insignificant as possible. She was breathless with excitement and her heart was hammering like crazy. It was Tuesday afternoon, and the girls had rushed home from school to put their plan to meet Isabella Duval into action.

Becky peeped through the glass doors at the scene outside the hotel. There was a crowd of photographers waiting in a roped-off area, as well as a group of fans who'd obviously found out somehow that Isabella was arriving today. James, the hotel doorman, was also waiting attentively for Isabella's car to appear.

'That's brilliant, Jas,' Becky had said approvingly when Jas had finished outlining her plan. 'But it'll have to be organized to the very *second* if it's going to work.'

'Well, if anyone can do that, you can, Becks,' Jas had pointed out. 'It'll be more like a military operation! But don't forget this is supposed to be fun too . . .'

Since Saturday, Becky had gone through the plan in her head over and over again, day and night. It *seemed* pretty foolproof. Jas had reminded the girls that whenever a guest stayed in the luxury Ruby, Diamond, Sapphire or Emerald suites on the top floor of the hotel, Lauren's dad always sent up a welcome drink just after they'd checked in.

'So how about if *we* take an *unofficial* drink up to Isabella before the *real* one arrives?' Jas had suggested, her dark eyes dancing with glee.

'Great idea,' Mia had agreed. 'But we'll have to time it perfectly in order to get there before the bar staff do.'

'We can do that,' Becky had said confidently. 'But we need to make sure no one guesses what we're up to, so that Lauren doesn't get into any trouble.'

'Thanks, guys,' Lauren had said gratefully. 'I can just imagine The Snoop's face if she found out what we were plotting!'

Impatiently Becky peered out through the glass doors again, but there was still no sign of

Isabella's car. Suddenly, though, she saw Lauren's dad come out of his office, straightening his tie. Becky slipped discreetly out of sight behind a large potted palm, and her heart began to thump even harder as Mr Bond hurried over to the hotel doors. He'd obviously had a message to say that Isabella Duval was on her way . . .

A few moments later, a sleek black limo drew up outside the hotel steps, and the fans erupted into loud cheers and whoops. Becky felt so excited, she couldn't stop her knees from shaking. She edged out slightly from behind the palm and fixed her gaze on the car.

James had opened the door and was helping Isabella Duval out. Becky caught her breath as she got her first glimpse of the world-famous star. Isabella was very slender and slight, and was somewhat shorter in real life than she looked on-screen, Becky realized. But she was just as beautiful, with her very long, very dark hair and her tanned, golden skin. She wore a floaty maxi-dress in shades of pink and lilac and very high-heeled, strappy, pale lilac shoes. She looked stunning, Becky thought dreamily.

Isabella smiled warmly as she posed on the steps for pictures. There were more cheers from the fans, who were now waving their autograph books, trying to attract Isabella's attention, while the photographers' flashguns blazed away as they shot picture after picture of the star. As Lauren's dad hurried forward to welcome the actress and her companion, a man in a dark-grey suit, Becky gave herself a mental shake. This was it! Time to put their plan into action . . .

Mr Bond was now escorting Isabella up the steps to the hotel doors, the actress stopping to sign autographs along the way. As James opened the glass doors to admit them, Becky hit a button on her mobile to call Lauren. Now it was up to Lauren and Jas to sort out the next phase of the plan, Becky thought, peeping out from behind the palm to get a closer look at Isabella as she passed by . . .

'Right, Jas, Becky's just buzzed me,' Lauren whispered. 'Here we go!'

If there's a mystery to solve . . . ask the girls from Mayfair Park
Look out for:
THE CASE of the Ruby Necklace
And coming Summer 2011
THE CASE of the Suspicious Supermodel

# bindi babes

## by Narinder Dhami

***Meet the coolest chicks on the block . . .***

These girls have been through tough times,
but now that they've got their perfect world sorted,
the one fashion accessory they don't need is an
interfering live-in auntie trying to cramp their style.

Bring on the collective power of the Bindi Babes!
Nothing in life, not even their formidable auntie-ji,
can stop these sisters . . . can it?

**'A fresh voice and fun characters that girls will love'**
***Jacqueline Wilson***

978 0 440 86512 4